His Amish Teacher

Patricia Davids

D0008978

 HARLEQUIN® LOVE INSPIRED®

Recycling programs
for this product may
not exist in your area.

LOVE INSPIRED BOOKS

ISBN-13: 978-0-373-62261-0

His Amish Teacher

Copyright © 2017 by Patricia MacDonald

Bear ye one another's burdens,
and so fulfill the law of Christ.
— *Galatians* 6:2

This book is dedicated to the memory of Joan Stroda. Heaven gained a dear and wonderful angel when she left this earth. Miss you, Mom. Love you still.

Chapter One

"We all know Teacher Lillian is a terrible cook, don't we, children?"

Lillian Keim's students erupted into giggles and some outright laugher. She crossed her arms and pressed her lips together to hold back a smile.

Timothy Bowman winked at her to take any sting out of his comment, but she wasn't offended. They had been friends for ages and were members of the same Amish community in Bowmans Crossing, Ohio. She knew he enjoyed a good joke as well as the next fellow, but he was deadly serious about his job today and so was she. The lessons they were presenting might one day prevent a tragedy.

He stood in front of her class on the infield of the softball diamond behind the one-room Amish schoolhouse where she taught all eight grades. Dressed in full fireman's turnout gear, Timothy made an impressive figure. The coat and pants added bulk to his slender frame, but he carried the additional weight with ease. His curly brown hair was hidden under a yellow helmet instead of his usual straw hat, but his hazel eyes sparkled with mirth. A smile lifted one side of his mouth and deepened the dimples in his tanned cheeks. Timothy smiled a lot. It was one reason she liked him.

His bulky fire coat and pants with bright fluorescent yellow banding weren't Plain clothing, but their Amish church district approved their use because the church elders and the bishop recognized the need for Amish volunteers to help fill the ranks of the local non-Amish fire company. The county fire marshal understood the necessity of special education in the Amish community where open flames and gas lanterns were used regularly. The Amish didn't allow electricity in their homes. Biannual fire-safety classes were held at all the local Amish schools. This was Timothy's first time giving the class. With Lillian's permission, he was deviating from the normal script with a demonstration outside. Timothy wanted to make an impression on the children. She admired that.

It was another unusually warm day for the last week of September. It had been a dry, hotter than usual summer. Timothy had chosen the bare dirt of the infield with an eye to safety rather than setting up on the brown grass of the lawn that could catch fire. The children were seated on the ground in a semicircle facing him. Only two of her older students, cousins Abe and Gabriel Mast, weren't paying attention. Abe was elbowing his cousin and the two were snickering and whispering behind their hands.

A red car sped past the school, and the driver laid on the horn. Abe jumped to his feet and waved wildly. The car didn't slow down.

Lillian did a double take. Was that her brother Jeremiah in the front passenger seat? Surely not. The vehicle rounded the sharp bend in the road and was gone from sight before she could be certain.

Abe grinned from ear to ear and kept jumping. "That's Davey's new ride. He's gonna teach me to drive, too. I want to go fast, fast, fast!"

Davey Mast was Abe's eldest brother. Davey had chosen to leave the Amish faith after his baptism and had been shunned for his decision. He had taken a job with a local *Englisch* farmer instead of leaving the area as most young people did when they didn't remain Amish. Lillian hoped her brother hadn't been in the car. If he had been, Jeremiah ran the risk of being shunned, too.

Abe ran toward the road. She called him back. "Abe, come sit down."

He ignored her.

"You need to pay attention. This is important." Timothy spoke sharply and leveled a stern look at Abe. The boy sheepishly returned to the group and sat down. Lillian wished she could use *the look* with the same effectiveness.

Timothy turned to a long table he had fashioned from wooden planks on a pair of sawhorses. A propane cook stove in the center held two pans that were both smoking hot. Various household items were arranged along the table, and a large pail of water sat on the ground in front of the table along with a red fire extinguisher.

He carefully carried one pan to the end of the table. Using a long-handled lighter, he clicked it once and the pan burst into flames. He looked at the children. "Let's pretend Teacher Lillian is frying chicken and a pan full of hot grease catches fire when no one else is around. What should you do?"

"Throw water on it," little Carl Mast shouted. The second grader was Abe's youngest brother.

"Carl says water will put out the fire. Let's see if that works." Timothy picked up a glass and filled it with water from a bucket beside the table. He flipped down the face shield of his helmet and tossed the liquid onto the skillet.

With a wild hiss and roar, the fire shot skyward in a flaming mushroom eight feet high. All the children drew back with wide frightened eyes. Lillian jumped, too. She wasn't expecting such a fireball. Puddles of burning grease dotted the ground.

Timothy lifted his face shield and looked at Carl. "Water isn't the right thing for putting out a grease fire, is it?"

Carl slowly shook his head, his eyes still wide.

Timothy used the extinguisher to put out the fires; then he lit the second pan ablaze with his lighter. "What is a safe way to put out a grease fire like this? Gabriel, Abe? What would you do? Quick. What's in the kitchen that will help?"

"I'd run outside and watch the whole thing go up in smoke," Abe said with a smirk, and elbowed his cousin. Gabriel nodded.

Timothy's eyes narrowed. "Not a very good answer, Abe. This isn't a joking matter."

"I'd get the fire extinguisher," Gabriel said quickly.

Timothy pointed to him. "*Goot.* Where is it kept in your home?"

A puzzled expression replaced Gabriel's grin. "I'm not sure."

Lillian calmly walked to the table. "A fine bunch of

firefighters you are if you can't put out a simple grease fire without help."

She picked up a dish towel, soaked it with water and gently draped it over the pan. The fire was instantly smothered. The children cheered.

Timothy nodded in appreciation. "I see Teacher Lillian has had lots of practice putting out her burning chicken. She did it the correct way. She smothered it. How else could she have smothered a grease fire?"

The children began calling out suggestions. He acknowledged each answer with a nod and a comment if it was a good suggestion. If it wasn't, he explained why. As he spoke, Lillian noticed he held the attention of all the children now. He had a knack for engaging them.

Timothy laid aside his lighter. "Now let's imagine that Teacher is burning leaves in the fall and she sees her *boo-friend* driving past." Again, the children giggled.

Lillian scowled at him, not amused this time. Timothy continued speaking. "She is so busy waving at him that she doesn't notice the hem of her dress has caught fire."

Sending him a sour look, she said, "I don't have a boyfriend, but I would certainly wave if one of my scholars were to pass by my home."

He wiped the grin off his face. "All right, one of your students has distracted you and now your hem is on fire."

She raised her arms in mock horror and shouted, "This is terrible! Help!"

"What should she do?" Timothy cupped one hand to his ear and leaned toward the children.

"Stop, drop and roll," the group yelled.

Lillian covered her face with both hands, dropped to the ground and rolled back and forth. She lifted her hand from her face and squinted at Timothy. "Did I do that right?"

He looked at the children. "Scholars, did Teacher Lillian do it correctly?"

"Ja!" they shouted in unison.

He held out his hand to help her up, his eyes sparkling. "Exactly right, Teacher."

She took his offered hand. His firm grip sent an unexpected rush of pleasure spiraling through her. As soon as she was on her feet, she pulled her hand from his and brushed at her dusty dress. "Next time you can do the stop, drop and roll while I ask the questions."

He grinned. "But you did it so well. You were far more graceful than I could ever be."

Turning to the children, she said, "Let's all thank Timothy for taking the time to teach us about fire safety."

"Thank you, Timothy," they said in unison.

Hannah added, *"Danki, Onkel* Timothy." Hannah was the stepdaughter of Timothy's brother, Joshua. Lillian tried hard not to have favorites, but she couldn't help it where Hannah was concerned.

"We only speak English at school, Hannah," Lillian reminded her.

Hannah ducked her head. "Sorry, Teacher. I forgot. Thank you, Uncle Timothy."

Lillian softened her tone. "It's all right. Sometimes I forget, too. Now, let's review some of the points Timothy made. Susan, can you tell us how often to change the batteries in our smoke detectors?"

"Twice a year, and the detectors should be replaced if they are more than seven years old," the eighth-grade girl said quickly, proving she had been listening. Susan

Yoder was one of Lillian's best students. The girl hoped to become a teacher someday.

Lillian gestured to Timothy's niece in the front row. "Hannah, what are some ways to prevent fires?"

Hannah wasn't a bit shy. She shot to her feet. "Don't ever play with matches. I don't, but Carl does."

Seated beside Hannah, the young boy leaned away from her and scowled. "Not anymore."

"I'm glad to hear that," Timothy said, a smile twitching at the corner of his lips.

Lillian raised her hand. "How many of you have practiced a fire escape plan with your family at home?" Nearly all the students raised their hands. Abe didn't and neither did his little brother Carl.

"All right, I want you to go inside, take out a piece of paper and draw a diagram of your home. I want you to show at least two ways to escape from the house in the event of a fire and mark where your meeting place is outside. Siblings may work together on the project."

The children rose and filed toward the school. Lillian stopped Susan. The girl served as Lillian's much-needed teacher's aide. "Will you help Hannah with this project? She doesn't have older siblings."

"Sure." Susan smiled and followed the others.

Abe shoved past Hannah, almost knocking her down when they reached the steps at the same time.

"Sorry," he said quickly, but he didn't sound remorseful in the least. He caught Gabriel's eye and whispered something to him. They both laughed as they went in.

Timothy moved to stand beside Lillian. "I noticed the son of our school board president is a bit of a troublemaker."

"Abe is, but I don't treat him differently because of his father."

Silas Mast, the school board president, had brushed aside her concerns about Abe's behavior when she tried to speak to him about it. His lack of support was making it more difficult to handle the boy.

Lillian watched until the last student entered the building; then she whirled to face Timothy with her hands on her hips. "What possessed you to suggest in front of my students that I have a boyfriend?"

He looked taken aback. "I didn't mean anything by it. I was making a point that you were distracted."

"You should have chosen better."

"Are you upset with me?"

She crossed her arms over her chest. "*Ja*, Timothy Bowman, I'm upset with you."

He relaxed. "*Nee*, you aren't. I can tell by the look in your eyes."

"How do my eyes look when I'm upset?" she demanded.

"Frosty."

Did he really know her so well? "And how do they look now?"

"Like you're trying to be serious, but you're smiling inside."

He was right, but she wasn't about to admit it.

He leaned one hip against the table. "How did I do for my first time giving a program?"

"Very well. You clearly have a knack for teaching."

"*Danki*. I tried to think about what I would say to my own children."

"Do you have a mother in mind for them?" she asked with false sweetness, knowing he was a single fellow.

She had heard a bit of gossip about him and wondered if it was true. Courting relationships were often closely guarded secrets in the Amish community.

He shook a finger at her. "Lillian Keim, you're prying."

She spread her hands wide. "You brought up the subject of children."

"I want a wife and children *someday*. I pray I will have sons to work beside me in our business as I have worked beside my father. I hope I may teach all my children to be good and faithful members of our church." His voice had grown soft. Lillian realized he was sharing something important with her.

"I hope God answers your prayers." A family of her own was something she would never have.

He tipped his head to the side as he regarded her. "What about you? How many children do you want?"

She gave a laugh but knew it sounded forced. "I have forty-one children to care for. That's more than enough. There will be forty-four next month because we have a new family transferring to our school. I hope the school board approves the hiring of a second teacher when they meet next Friday. I'm not sure I can manage that many."

"Still, you must want children of your own someday."

That wasn't possible. Only her parents knew about the surgery that had saved her life but left her barren. She'd never told anyone else. She didn't want pity. God had chosen this path for her. It wasn't an easy one, but she would do her best to live as He willed.

She drew a steadying breath and raised her chin. "Every morning I wake up and think about these children waiting for me and I can't wait to get here. I thank God every day and night for leading me to this work. I love it. Are you shocked that I want a career instead of a family?"

"*Nee*, I'm not. Luke mentioned as much to me."

"You and your brother were talking about me?"

"It was last Christmas. Luke thought the reason I was helping with the school program was that I wanted to court you. He decided to become my unofficial go-between and have Emma find out if you would be interested in dating me. Emma told him you were devoted to teaching and not looking to marry. He relayed that to me."

"And was that the reason behind your offer to help at the school?"

Timothy shook his head. "You and the *kinder* needed help. Friends help friends."

A touch of disappointment pricked her, but she quickly suppressed it. She valued his friendship. Any sign of romantic attachment from either of them would make their friendship awkward and could bring censure down on her. As a teacher, she was expected to be a model of proper behavior. "Your help made the program extra special. *Danki*."

He shrugged off her praise. "I didn't do much."

Now it was her turn to tease him. Checking to make sure they wouldn't be overheard, she leaned closer. "I understand you are Nellie Martin's come-calling friend. Is it serious?"

His eyebrows shot up. "What? Who told you that?"

"You were seen driving together last Sunday evening."

"I passed Nellie walking along the road after visiting her sister and I gave her a lift home because I was going the same way. That's all. I'm not her come-calling friend or anyone else's, for that matter."

"See how easily rumors get started?" She was glad he wasn't seeing anyone. When he did find the right woman, Lillian knew their friendship would change.

A gleam sparkled in the depths of his eyes. He leaned toward her. "Would you be jealous if I were going out with her, Teacher?"

Trust him to turn the tables on her. "Of course not, but rumors will soon circulate that I have a new *boo-friend*."

"Why?"

"Because these forty-one students will go home and repeat what they learned today. Some of them will fail to mention you were teasing about my boyfriend. By Sunday after the prayer meeting I'll be answering carefully worded questions from many curious mothers as they try to figure out who he might be."

A frown line appeared on his forehead. "Do you really think so? I didn't mean to make trouble."

"I know small children and the way they can mix up the simplest things. When people start asking, I'm going to tell everyone it's you."

He pressed his hands over his heart. "Teacher, don't get my hopes up unless you mean it."

It was her turn to frown. "What is that supposed to mean?"

"I would be your *boo-friend* in a heartbeat. May I come courting?"

Chapter Two

Timothy watched an array of fleeting expressions cross Lillian's delicate face. Surprise, dismay and finally skepticism narrowed her green eyes. He would cheerfully snatch back his words if he could. She had to know he was joking, didn't she? Had he gone too far this time?

Her eyes narrowed. "Where is that bucket of water? You need to soak your head."

"Is that any way to talk to the man you're dating?"

She jabbed her finger into his chest. "I'm too smart to go out with you, and it's nothing to joke about."

"You are right. Courting and marriage are not joking matters." Relieved that he hadn't truly upset her, he turned the conversation in a safer direction. "What did you think of the book I lent you?"

Her tense shoulders relaxed at his change of subject. "I haven't had time to sit down with it yet."

"Teacher hasn't finished her homework. Shame on you."

"I do have papers to grade and lessons to prepare."

"I will accept that excuse today, but I'm dying to

know if you find the story as funny as I did. The main character reminded me of you."

"I thought you said it was about a dog."

"It is. A lovable, devoted dog who believes she knows what's best for every creature in the barnyard. Truly, it's a great book with an excellent message."

"So I'm like a bossy dog, is that what you are saying?"

She rolled her eyes, and he chuckled. He enjoyed teasing Lillian. They had been close friends when they were younger, drawn together by a love of books and reading. He cherished the hours they had spent discussing the works of Dickens, Henry David Thoreau and the stories of their persecuted Amish ancestors in *The Martyr's Mirror*. His love of reading was something his brothers never understood.

Lillian and her family had moved away the summer he turned eighteen. He'd lost touch with her for a few years, but he never forgot the way she made him feel. The Amish valued hard work. Book learning had its place, but few people understood his desire to read and learn more about the world the way Lillian did.

When she returned to the area after six years away, he had been delighted but his first efforts to rekindle their friendship had been rebuffed. Lillian had changed while she was away. She had become remote and reserved. It had taken a great deal of patience on his part to repair the bond between them.

Besides helping with the Christmas program, he had done what handiwork was needed at the school without being asked. He sometimes bought books for the school library and occasionally suggested a new novel he thought she might like. His diligence over the course of the winter had slowly thawed her reserve. Now that they were enjoying an easy comradery again, he would do his best to keep it that way.

"Looks like you have a visitor," he said, gesturing to the road where a white car was pulling up to a stop on the narrow road in front of the school.

Lillian shaded her eyes as she gazed that way. A young woman got out of the car. She went to the back and opened the trunk.

"Do you know her?" Timothy asked.

"I had a letter from the public health department telling me Miss Debra Merrick would be here to do health screenings on the children today."

The woman closed the trunk of her car and picked up two large black cases.

"I'd better go help her with those bags. They look heavy."

He judged Debra to be near his age, somewhere in her midtwenties. She was dressed modern in a simple blue skirt and a white blouse with lace at her throat. Her black shoes were low-heeled and sensible, but they sported shiny buckles that wouldn't be acceptable in his Plain community. Her blond hair was cut short and floated in curls around her face.

He glanced at Lillian. Amish women never cut their hair. They kept it covered beneath a white prayer *kapp* like the one Lillian wore. The white ribbons of her bonnet fluttered softly in the breeze and drew his gaze to the slender curve of her neck. What would her hair look like if she wore it down? He could imagine it spilling in rich brown waves down her back. Would it reach the floor? He jerked his gaze away. It wasn't proper to think such thoughts about a friend. He focused on the woman beside the car.

"Can I give you a hand with those?" he asked as he and Lillian drew near.

"Thank you. That's very kind." She put the cases down and smiled sweetly as she tucked a curl behind her ear.

Lillian held out her hand. "I'm Lillian Keim, the teacher here. This is Timothy Bowman."

"I'm Debra Merrick." The woman shook hands with both of them.

"I was expecting you early this morning," Lillian said.

Debra flushed a rosy shade of pink. "I'm afraid I got lost on these winding rural roads. Twice."

Timothy began undoing his coat. "It happens. We aren't exactly in the middle of nowhere, but you can see it from here."

Debra's gaze carried a hint of gratitude for his understanding. She gestured toward the smoking pans on the table. "Has there been a fire?"

He chuckled as he pulled his helmet off and combed his fingers through his damp curls. "Only a fire safety demonstration. I'll bring your cases up to the school once I shed this gear."

He stepped over to his wagon, undid the heavy coat and tossed it along with his helmet on the wooden bench seat. He picked up his straw hat and settled it on his head.

Turning around, he saw Miss Merrick watching him with a look of surprise on her face. "You're Amish? I didn't know the Amish could be firemen."

He laughed heartily. "Then I reckon there's a lot you don't know about us Amish folk."

She gave him a sheepish smile. "I'm afraid that's true. My family has some Amish ancestry, but this is my first visit to Amish country and my first Amish school to visit."

"We are more than farmers and quilters. You'll find we're a lot like everyone else if you take the time to get to know us," he added.

"I'm always willing to learn new things, and I like getting to know new people."

He nodded once. *"Goot."*

Debra tipped her head to the side. "What does that mean?"

"It means good. It's Pennsylvania *Deitsch*. You might have heard it called Pennsylvania Dutch, although it's not Dutch at all. It's an old German dialect."

Her smile widened. *"Goot.* I'll remember that. Thank you for teaching me something new today, Mr. Bowman."

She seemed like a sweet woman. "Call me Timothy."

"All right, Timothy."

Lillian stepped between them and shot him a stern, frosty look before she turned to Debra. "Come up to the school and meet the children, Miss Merrick. They've been waiting for you."

Timothy stared after Lillian in puzzlement. What was *that* look for?

Lillian resisted the urge to grab Timothy by the collar and shake him. Didn't he realize the woman was boldly flirting with him and that he was encouraging her? Outsiders were to be dealt with cautiously. Timothy's behavior bordered on prideful. Being forward or asserting oneself in any way was contrary to their church's teachings and he knew that.

Once they were inside the school, she directed Debra

to a table at the back of the room to set up her equipment. Timothy placed the cases next to it. Lillian welcomed the health screening and other educational health programs presented by the local public health department. Each year her students received dental and eye exams as well as hearing screenings and classes on the hazards of tobacco use and smoking, all free of charge.

Debra looked over the room and spoke softly to Lillian. "I'm afraid I'm not going to get all the children done today. I don't want to keep them after school. Would it be all right if I return tomorrow?"

"That won't be a problem. School starts at eight o'clock."

Debra let out a sigh of relief. "That will be great. Now that I know the way, I should be here on time. On a personal note, I was hoping to purchase some authentic Amish-made gifts for my friends back home. Can you suggest somewhere to shop locally?"

"My mother runs a gift shop just over the river," Timothy said. "You passed it before you came through the covered bridge. You'll find everything there is reasonably priced and all handmade. If you'd like to see some Amish-made furniture, I'd be happy to show you around my father's woodworking shop."

"I'd like that very much. I'll stop by after I finish here tomorrow."

"Great. I'll see you then."

"Maybe you can teach me a few more Amish words." She gave him a sly smile and a wink.

"I've recently been told I have a knack for teaching."

He looked so smug that Lillian was tempted to kick his shin. She forced herself to remain polite. "We should let Miss Merrick get to work, Timothy. I'll help you clean up outside."

"It was nice meeting you, Debra." He nodded to her and went out the door. Lillian followed him to the make-shift table and checked the pans to see if they were cool enough to handle.

"Are you going to tell me what's wrong?" he asked.

"Nothing's wrong." Was it her place to correct his behavior? Her father would say it was.

"You've been giving me your *frosty* stare ever since Miss Merrick arrived."

"If you want to make puppy eyes at the *Englisch* lady, I'm sure it's none of my business."

He frowned as he snatched up the water pail. "I wasn't making puppy eyes at her."

"Ha! If you had a tail, it would have been wagging a mile a minute the second she smiled at you."

"How can you say that?"

"I say it because it's true."

"I was being *nice*. She seems like a very pleasant lady. Which is more than I can say for you at the moment." He threw the water out, picked up the fire extinguisher and headed for his wagon.

Lillian nibbled on the corner of her lip as she watched him stomp away. He was right. She wasn't being pleasant, and she had no right to chastise him. He hadn't broken any church rules. Friendliness with outsiders wasn't forbidden, just discouraged. She wasn't sure why it upset her to see him so at ease with the woman.

Timothy came back and carried a pair of sawhorses past her without comment. He set them in the back of the wagon. It was clear he was upset with her and that wasn't like Timothy.

"I'm sorry if I offended you," she said.

"You have." He brushed past her to pick up the last of the boards and carried them to the wagon, too. He threw them in and they clattered loudly. The horses shifted uneasily at the noise but quickly settled at a low word from him.

Lillian took a step closer. "I'm only looking out for your best interests. Your behavior could be seen as forward and unacceptable. I'm sorry if pointing that out makes you angry."

He leaned a hip against the wagon and folded his arms over his chest as he fixed his gaze on her face. "That you judge my behavior to be forward and unacceptable is what makes me angry. I thought you knew me well enough to know I wouldn't flirt with any woman, let alone someone who didn't share our faith."

She clutched her arms tight across her chest. "I do know that."

"Then why accuse me of it?"

She stared at her feet and tried to put her feelings into words. "You smiled at her."

"I smile at everyone."

"I know, but she smiled back. I saw that look in her eyes."

"What are you talking about? What look?"

Lillian glanced at his handsome face. "The look that said she was interested in getting to know you better. A lot better."

He shook his head in disbelief. "I'm not responsible for the way someone looks at me."

"I saw the attraction between the two of you. Such feelings can lead you down a forbidden path."

He threw his hands in the air. "I can't believe I'm

hearing this. I had no idea you thought I was so weak-minded."

"I don't." The last thing she wanted was for him to be angry with her.

"Your words say otherwise, Lillian."

He climbed in his wagon. With a slap of the reins, he headed his horses down the road, leaving her to watch his rapidly retreating figure and regret her ill-advised comments. They'd never had a disagreement, let alone an argument like this.

Had she damaged their friendship beyond repair?

Chapter Three

Drawing a deep calming breath, Lillian returned to the schoolroom determined to be pleasant to Miss Merrick. She would apologize to Timothy soon. Perhaps she could think of an excuse to visit the Bowman household after school tonight and find a way to speak to Timothy alone. And then again, maybe she was being foolish. Their friendship was surely strong enough to weather one disagreement. Wasn't it? She didn't need to run after him and beg his forgiveness.

Inside the school, she helped Debra set up the eye charts. Together, they taped off the correct distance on the floor where the children were to stand. Suddenly, the outside door burst open, and Lillian's little sister Amanda raced in.

Spying Lillian, the four-year-old dashed across the room and threw her arms around Lillian's legs. "*Shveshtah*, I *koom* to visit you at *schule*. Teach me something?"

Tiny for her age, Amanda had been born with dwarfism. Her arms and legs were short, but her body was near normal in size. Her blond hair was fine and straight as wheat straw with wisps of it peeking from beneath her white *kapp*.

Lillian scooped the child up in her arms and settled her at her hip. "The first thing my scholars learn is to be quiet in the classroom. No shouting. No running."

Amanda's smile faded. "I was bad, wasn't I?"

Lillian nodded. "A little."

The outside door opened again and Lillian's father, Eldon Keim, came in, his face set in stern lines. Something must be wrong.

Miss Merrick gave Amanda a bright smile. "Is this your daughter?"

"Amanda is my sister." Lillian introduced her father to Miss Merrick.

"I'm very pleased to meet you, Mr. Keim, and you, Amanda." Debra held out her hand to the child.

Amanda shyly shook it.

Debra's smile widened. "I have a brother who is a little person. His name is Brandon. He has cartilage-hair hypoplasia."

A rush of empathy caused Lillian to look kindly at Debra. Here was someone who understood the challenging life her little sister faced. "That is exactly what Amanda has."

"I mentioned my family has Amish ancestors. I'm sure you know CCH is one of the more common types of dwarfism among the Amish. I wish Brandon could meet Amanda. He loves children, especially little-people children. He and his wife have adopted two children with dwarfism. He's a professor of agriculture at Ohio Central University. I know that sounds like a stuffy job, but he's not a bit stuffy."

Her father spoke quietly in Pennsylvania Dutch. "I'm

going into town. Your mother said you needed something."

"*Ja*, I have two library books that are due back today. Can you drop them off for me?" It would save her a long walk this evening. Bless her mother for thinking of it.

"Fetch them quickly."

She put Amanda down, hurried to her desk and returned with both volumes. *"Danki."*

He scanned the titles and frowned. "Are these proper reading for an Amish woman?"

Lillian was glad he'd kept the conversation in Pennsylvania *Deitsch*. It stung that he didn't trust her judgment, but as a minister of the church, he had to make sure his family obeyed the *Ordnung*, the rules of the church. The books were teaching guides for elementary science, a subject she struggled to understand and teach. "They were recommended to me at the last teachers' conference I attended. What's wrong, *Daed*?"

He tucked the books under his arm. "I received a letter today from my sister in Wisconsin. My *onkel* Albert is gravely ill and wishes to see me. We are leaving tonight. I must speak with the bishop and let him know I won't be preaching with him on Sunday."

"I'm so sorry. Is Amanda going with you?"

"Nee, your mother and I think it best she stay at home with you and Jeremiah. Can she spend the rest of the afternoon with you today?"

Lillian winked at Amanda. "She isn't old enough to start school."

"If it is a problem, she can come with me to the bishop's home," he said.

Amanda's eyes widened, and she shook her head. The bishop was a kindly man, but his stern countenance and booming voice had frightened the child once and she remained leery of him.

Planting her hands on her hips, Lillian pretended to consider the situation, then finally nodded and smiled. "*Ja*, she can stay with me."

After her father left, Debra took a tentative step closer. "Is something wrong?"

Realizing Debra hadn't understood their exchange, Lillian explained. "My father has been called to his uncle's deathbed in Wisconsin. He and my mother must make arrangements to travel there as soon as possible."

"They can't go that far by horse and buggy, can they?"

"They will hire a driver to take them. We are not allowed to own cars, but we are not forbidden to ride in them. Many local people earn extra money by driving their Amish neighbors when there is a need."

"I see. I'm sorry your father's uncle is so ill." Debra laid a hand on Lillian's shoulder. Lillian was surprised by the sincere sympathy in her eyes.

"He has lived a long full life." Lillian recalled with fondness her great-uncle's gnarled hands and his toothless grin. He kept a tall glass jar by his chair and he always had a licorice twist to share with her and his many grandchildren and great-grandchildren. It was sad to think of his passing, but she knew he was ready to go home.

Debra stepped back. "I should get to work. Will the children have trouble understanding me? I know you speak a different language."

"Only the youngest will have trouble. Start with the upper grades today. They have all had eye exams before."

Lillian settled Amanda on a seat by her desk and gave her several picture books to look at while she finished grading the spelling tests from the day before. Debra was only halfway through the eye exams when it was time to dismiss for the day.

Lillian looked out over the classroom. "Put your books away and quietly get your coats."

Abe and Gabriel rushed to the cloakroom and then dashed out the door before she could stop them. She couldn't very well chase after them. She would have to deal with their disrespectful attitude tomorrow. This couldn't continue.

She walked to the door and held it open. "Children, you are dismissed."

The rest of the children filed outside in an orderly manner that lasted only until they reached the final step on the porch. After that, they bolted like young colts being let out to pasture. Childish laughter and shouts filled the air as they said goodbye to each other and to her. For Lillian, there was always a sense of relief followed by a small letdown when they were gone from her sight. They were hers for seven hours each day, but none of them belonged to her.

Thankfully, she had Amanda. Her baby sister was as close as Lillian would ever come to having a child of her own. She looked toward her desk and saw Amanda was sharing her picture book with Debra.

"What is this?" Debra asked, pointing to the page. She had taken a seat on the floor by the child's chair.

Amanda said, *"Dess ist ein gaul."*

"Gaul. That must mean horse. Am I right?" Debra looked to Lillian for confirmation. She nodded.

"And this?" Debra pointed to the page again.

"Hund."

"So dog is *hund.*"

Amanda grinned and turned the page. She pointed and said, *"Hohna."*

"Chicken is *hohna*." Debra giggled as she stumbled over the unfamiliar word.

"Hohna means rooster." Lillian sat in her chair and scooted closer to Amanda so she could see the pictures, too.

Amanda pointed to the drawing of a hen sitting on a nest of straw. *"Glukk."*

"That has got to mean chicken." Debra glanced at Lillian.

"Not exactly. It means a sitting hen, one who lays eggs."

"Goot, glukk, hohna, hund, gaul. Good, sitting hen, rooster, dog, horse. I've learned a pocketful of new words today. Thank you, Amanda. I shall thoroughly impress Mr. Bowman with my new vocabulary when I see him tomorrow."

Lillian's smile faded. She spoke quietly in *Deitsch* to her sister. "Put your things away. You may go outside and play on the swings until I'm ready to go home."

The child got up without further prompting. She put her colors and book away, and headed out the door.

"She's very sweet," Debra said.

"She is a great blessing to me and to my entire family."

"I'm glad to hear you say that. Children with special needs aren't always seen as a blessing." Debra's tone held a touch of bitterness that surprised Lillian.

"The Amish believe handicapped children are extraordinary gifts from God. A family with such a child faces difficulties, yes, but they know God has smiled upon them in a very special way."

"I wish my family held such a belief. My father saw my brother as a burden and wondered what he had done wrong to be cursed with a deformed son."

"I'm sorry for your father. I pray he comes to see the error in his way of thinking."

"He passed away a few years ago. I think in the end he came to accept Brandon as a gift, but growing up, my brother faced prejudices from inside and outside of our home. I'm amazed he has turned out as normal and happy as he seems to be."

"We have a proverb about our children. *The more a child is valued, the better his values will be.*"

"You are making me sorry my great-great-grandfather left the Amish. May I ask you something personal?"

Lillian thought their conversation was already personal, but she nodded.

"I had the feeling that you were upset after my arrival today. Did I do something wrong? I don't want to alienate you or others in this community. If I did do something unacceptable, please tell me. I won't be offended. I plan to begin teaching adult education classes in this area on health and food safety later this fall, and I know I need to learn more about your Amish ways if I'm to be effective."

Lillian looked down at her hands. "I was upset, and I beg your forgiveness for that. It wasn't your behavior, so much as the behavior of Timothy Bowman that upset me."

"His behavior? I found him incredibly friendly and very sweet. What did he do that upset you? He's a bit of a flirt, but that's harmless. Oh, unless you two are dating or something? That would put a totally different spin on it."

"Timothy and I are simply friends," she said quickly. Maybe too quickly. A hint of speculation widened Debra's eyes.

"He's a nice-looking fellow. Is he married?"

"Timothy is single."

"I notice you aren't wearing a wedding band. I take it you're single, too?"

"Amish women do not wear jewelry, even wedding rings, but I am single and I shall remain so. If I were to marry I would have to give up teaching."

"Really? That's very old-fashioned."

"We are an old-fashioned people. Becoming a wife and a mother is a sacred duty that must come before all else. Very few married Amish women work outside the home."

As an outsider, Lillian wasn't sure Debra would understand, but if she was going to be working in their community, she had to become informed about what was and was not acceptable. "You may have seen Timothy's behavior as harmless, but our church would take a very different view. We are to be meek before God and man, never drawing attention to ourselves or putting ourselves above others. We call it *demut*, humbleness."

"I think I see. I wouldn't consider Timothy's behavior humble, but it wasn't offensive."

"Timothy has a sweet nature, but his outgoing personality draws attention and that is frowned upon."

"I was told the Amish were cold and unwelcoming. I'm happy to say I have not found that to be true. Thank you for explaining this to me. I'll ignore Timothy's winsome ways and practice being modest and humble." Debra leaned toward Lillian and grinned. "I'm afraid *that* will be a hard task for me to master."

Lillian decided she liked this outsider. "We have another proverb that may help. *You can tell when you're on the right track because it's usually uphill.*"

"Care to share with us, *bruder* Timothy?"

Timothy looked up from contemplating the coffee in his white mug to find his brother Luke staring at him. He glanced around and found his little brother Noah, his mother and his father all staring at him as if waiting for him to speak. He had no idea what they had been discussing. Lillian's accusation had been the only thing on his mind since he left the school yesterday afternoon. Why had she accused him of flirting with the English lady? Her lack of trust chafed at his mind.

Knowing only she could answer his questions, he forced his attention back to his family. "I'm sorry. What were you talking about?"

Luke chuckled. "Who put a knot in your tail?"

Timothy knew better than to ignore Luke's teasing. It would only get worse if he did. "No one has put a knot in my tail. I was thinking about my fire safety class and how I could improve things." It wasn't the whole truth, but he hoped it would satisfy his sharp-eyed brother.

"I asked you how it went." His mother refilled his coffee cup from the pot sitting on a hot pad near her elbow and offered him the last cinnamon roll in the pan. Ana Bowman was happiest when she was feeding someone. He was surprised that they weren't all as plump as bullfrogs.

He nodded his thanks for the refill but passed on the roll. "I think it went well. For the most part, the children paid close attention. They sure are a bright bunch. No wonder Lillian enjoys teaching them."

Ana put the pan aside. "You impressed Hannah. She told me all about it when she came home yesterday. I'm dying to know who Lillian's boyfriend is. Do you know?"

Timothy cringed. He would be in hot water with Lillian now for sure. "She isn't seeing anyone. I made up a story about her having a boyfriend to show how she might become distracted, and…never mind. I can't believe Hannah repeated that. Lillian doesn't have a beau."

"Told you she didn't." Luke stuffed his last bite of cinnamon roll in his mouth and reached for the pan. "If Lillian was seeing someone, Emma would know."

"But would Emma tell you?" *Mamm* asked.

Their father pushed away from the table. "If we are done gossiping about our neighbors, perhaps we can get some work done today."

His sons heeded the annoyance in his tone and quickly finished their coffee. They followed him out the door and across the graveled yard to the woodworking shop. The sun was just peeking over the horizon. It promised to be another warm day. One of the horses whinnied at them from the corral. The cattle and horses in the big red barn had been fed well before the men sat down to breakfast.

In the large workshop, they were joined by several other carpenters. Timothy's oldest brother, Samuel, moved to stand beside their father with a clipboard in his hand. Everyone gathered around him awaiting instructions for the day.

Samuel flipped through the sheets of paper on his board. "We've received a new order for sixteen beds with carved headboards and footboards."

"Must be an order from an Amish family if they need

sixteen beds," Noah said under his breath to Luke and Timothy.

Timothy choked on a laugh. Luke nudged their little brother with his elbow. "The Amish aren't the only ones with big families."

Noah elbowed him back. "Tell that to *Mamm*. She expects us to give her a dozen grandchildren each. Or more."

A grin twitched at the corner of Samuel's mouth. "I'm doing my part."

He and his wife had welcomed a baby boy in May to the delight of everyone, especially Ana Bowman.

"This order comes from an inn being built in upstate New York," *Daed* said, clearly struggling to keep from laughing. They all knew Noah spoke the truth.

Timothy thought of his conversation with Lillian about children. He did want a big family. He wanted a devout wife to be his helpmate, to share his burdens and his joys. A woman who was bright and quick-thinking. Someone who loved bringing out the best in others the way Lillian did. While there were a few nice women he could date, none of them ignited the spark he expected to feel when the right woman came along.

"We are blessed to have the quality of our work recognized by someone so far away." Samuel pointed to Timothy. "You and Luke select the wood to be used. They want oak and walnut with pine as a secondary wood. You know the kind of lumber we need."

"Straight with no knots in it." Timothy was already thinking of the boards that were stacked beneath tarps behind the shop. The last delivery of locally cut walnut had been above average quality.

Samuel nodded. "Exactly. Joshua and Noah, I want

you to work on creating sixteen different but coordinated designs for the headboards. Each one has to represent an animal native to the northern woods. We have a list. Deer, moose, bobcat, bear, ducks, geese, raccoon, you get the idea." He handed the paper to Joshua.

"How about a skunk?" Noah suggested.

Samuel shook his head. "Are you ever serious?"

"Rarely."

Timothy spoke up. "I'm sure we can come up with sixteen that will satisfy the customer. How much time do we have to complete the order?"

Samuel flipped a paper over. "Ten weeks."

"Finally, an *Englisch* customer who isn't in a flat-out rush," Noah said.

His comment reminded Timothy that he had promised to show Debra around the shop after she was done at the school today. He had been happy to extend the invitation yesterday, but now he wished he hadn't. Lillian was sure to be upset if he spent more time with the pretty *Englisch* nurse.

Samuel handed Timothy a sheet of paper with the dimensions for the beds. He and Luke headed for the back door of the shop. A low beep made Luke stop and pull his fire department pager from his waistband. "Is it your turn to be on call or should I give it to Noah?"

"It's my turn. Does it need to be charged?" The family had a diesel generator to run the electric equipment in their business. A single outlet in their father's office was the only place the brothers could charge their pagers when the generators were running.

"*Ja*, it does. Wouldn't want you to miss a call. How many times have we gone out this month?"

"Eight." Twice as many as usual. Mostly rubbish fires

that had gotten out of hand, but one had been a large hay fire that threatened a house and barn. Fortunately, no one had been injured and the blaze had been contained.

Luke glanced out the door. "This warm weather and lack of rain has left the land as dry as tinder. I pray it rains soon."

"Amen to that." Timothy followed him outside and around the back of the building where a covered shed housed their lumber.

Once they were outside, Luke faced Timothy and planted his hands on his hips. "Now that no one else in the family is listening, what's really bothering you?"

So he hadn't fooled his eagle-eyed brother. "If you must know, Lillian accused me of flirting with the visiting nurse who came to the school yesterday. I wasn't flirting. I was being nice to the woman."

"Was this nurse a pretty woman?"

"I guess you could say that."

"And Lillian became upset because you were being nice to a pretty woman."

"Ja."

"Well, that explains a lot."

Timothy scowled at Luke. "Not to me, it doesn't. What do you know that I don't?"

"She's jealous."

"Lillian? You can't be serious. *Nee*, that isn't it."

"You and she are friends. Close friends. Right?"

"Since we were in third grade. Everyone knows that. So?"

"She has had your undivided devotion for years. Maybe she saw for the first time that she might not always be the center of your life. You two aren't children anymore."

Timothy mulled over his brother's words. Was Luke right? If he was, what did that mean for the relationship Timothy cherished?

Chapter Four

Early the next morning, Lillian rounded the sharp bend in the road and was surprised to see Debra sitting on the school steps. The sun was barely up in the east. A thin mist hugged the river and low places. Lillian knew it would burn off quickly when the sun rose in the sky.

The sight of the young woman brought back the memory of Lillian's quarrel with Timothy. Her family's hurried departure as well as her false pride had kept her from seeking him out yesterday. He deserved an apology. After school, she would make a point to seek him out. She cherished his friendship and didn't want to lose it.

"Good morning," Deborah called out cheerfully as she waved.

"Good morning. You certainly arrived early enough."

"I was determined to be on time this morning. I parked my car beside that empty shed over there. I hope that's okay."

"It's fine. In poor weather I drive my buggy and park inside, but as you can see, I walked today."

"How far away do you live?"

"Not far. Two and a half miles."

"I wouldn't like to hike that far for my job. I spent some time doing research last night that I should have done before coming here. I'm afraid I discovered more questions than answers. Is it true that Amish children don't go to school beyond the eighth grade?"

Lillian climbed the steps and held the door open for Debra. "It is true."

"Even you, a teacher?"

"You must find that shocking. We believe that beyond elementary school, vocational training is sufficient for Amish youth. Some cases of higher education are permitted. I earned my GED and took some college courses by correspondence before I was baptized into the faith. Admittedly, I'm something of an exception. Amish teachers rarely have more education than their students, but I knew I was preparing for a lifetime vocation."

"I can certainly understand that. What is the curriculum like here?"

"I teach the basics of reading, writing and arithmetic just as the majority of public schools did over a century ago. In addition, I teach German." Lillian laid her books and papers on her desk.

"I'm aware that in the case of Wisconsin versus Yoder in 1972, the United States Supreme Court ruled that Amish children could end their formal schooling at the age of fourteen. But getting a good education is so important in this day and age. I'm not sure I see how your children can prosper without it."

Picking up an eraser, Lillian began to wipe away her class assignments from the day before. "Education must prepare our children to be productive members of our community, not productive members of the greater world. I teach English because it is the language of our neighbors and of our commerce. A man cannot sell milk or goods if he doesn't understand what his customer is saying. I teach German because we use the Bible written in that language just as our ancestors did in our church services. My students also learn about health and basic science, although not all Amish schools are as progressive as we are. Each school board decides what is important and what is to be taught. In some areas of education, you may find us lacking, but we do what is best for our children and our way of life.

"I certainly didn't learn a new language in grade school."

Lillian realized how puffed up she must sound and turned to face Debra. "And I am guilty of pride. Please forgive me for lecturing you."

"As I have said before, I enjoy learning new things. Thank you for the lesson and you are forgiven if you will forgive my ignorance and not take offense at my many questions."

"That is a deal. We Amish are free to read and study ways to improve our lives as long as they do not go against the teaching of our church. We believe higher education puts our children at risk of exposure to worldly behaviors that we do not condone."

"But what about doctors and nurses? Don't the Amish want their own people in such professions?"

"There is a need for doctors and nurses, we don't deny that. We are grateful for the men and women who seek to serve mankind in such a fashion, but the core of our faith is that we must be separate from the world. In it, but not a part of it. We must forsake all self-interest and humbly submit to the authority of the church. To us, this is the only way to be righteous in the sight of God.

Any display of pride is a sin. If we take pride in being Amish, that, too, is a sin."

"I respect your right to believe as you wish, but I can't say that I understand it."

Lillian smiled. "I won't hold that against you."

She had never met anyone as forthright as Debra. The two previous health workers who had come to the school had been all business and not talkative in the least.

The sound of childish chatter outside signaled the arrival of her first students. Most were able to walk to the school, but a few were delivered to her doorstep in buggies driven by their parents or older siblings.

Debra glanced at the clock on the wall. It was five minutes until eight. "I need a quiet place for the hearing tests later today. Where do you suggest?"

"The cloakroom, or we have a basement if you'd like to see it."

"I think the cloakroom will work."

Lillian helped Debra move an unused desk and chair into the room. Outside, the sounds of children at play grew louder. The swings and the merry-go-round were favorite places for the students to play before school started.

Debra moved to the window. "They were so quiet yesterday, but they sound loud and rambunctious now. Maybe I should use the basement."

"Noise won't be a problem." Lillian went to the front steps.

Hannah ran up to her. "Teacher, *Mamm* brought me to school in our new pony cart. Isn't it pretty? That's our new pony. His name is Hank."

Lillian looked toward the road. Mary Bowman waved from the seat of a small two-wheeled wooden cart painted sky blue. A small black pony with a snip of white on his nose tossed his thick black mane. Lillian returned Mary's wave and turned to Hannah. "It's a very nice cart, and he looks like a fine pony."

"I made these for you." Hannah thrust a shoe box toward Lillian.

"How kind. What can it be?" Lillian's heart expanded with joy as she lifted the box to her ear and shook it. The rattle and aroma of gingersnaps gave her a hint. She peeked inside the lid. "Did you make these all by yourself? They look scrumptious."

"*Grossmammi* Ana helped me."

Lillian laid the box aside. "Please thank your grandmother Ana for me."

"We have something for you, too." Karen and Carla Beachy, third-grade twins, came up beside Hannah. They had each drawn a picture of their favorite cow named Willow. Lillian took the pictures and admired them. "These are lovely. I shall put them on the wall for everyone to enjoy."

"*Guder mariye*, Teacher." Carl Mast rushed up with a big grin.

"It is a beautiful morning." This was truly her favorite part of the day. More of her children greeted her and shared the news from home and she realized once again how truly blessed she was.

She rang the bell. Her students who were still playing outside immediately stopped what they were doing and filed quietly into the schoolhouse. They came in, put away their lunches and took their seats. Even Abe and Gabriel were quiet this morning.

Lillian stood in front of her desk. "Good morning, scholars."

"Good morning, Teacher," they said in unison.

"As you can see, Nurse Merrick has returned to finish your health screenings. You are to go with her when it is your turn."

Lillian moved to the blackboard that covered the front wall of the school and wrote out the date and the arithmetic assignments for each of the classes. When she finished, she picked up her Bible. Each day she chose a passage to read from the Old or the New Testament. This morning she chose 2 Corinthians 6. After the reading, her students rose, clasped their hands together and repeated the Lord's Prayer in unison.

Lillian picked up her copy of *Unpartheyisches Gesang-Buch*, their German songbook, from the corner of her desk. Singing was a normal part of each school day. Without being told, the children filed to the front of the room and lined up in their assigned places. She chose two English songs out of respect to their guest and one German hymn. Gabriel, the best singer in the school, began the hymn. The other children's voices rose together in unison as they sang without musical accompaniment. When the songs were finished, they all returned to their seats.

Susan Yoder began handing out readers to the three lower grades. The older students took out their arithmetic workbooks. All the children knew what was expected of them, and they did it without instructions. After Susan finished handing out the readers, she went with Debra to translate for the youngest ones being tested.

By ten o'clock, it was time for recess. Debra emerged from the cloakroom as the children surged around her to hurry outside. She came to the open door, where Lillian stood watching her charges. "I have to say that I'm amazed by how well behaved your students are. I hope every school I visit will be this cooperative."

Lillian smiled at her. "Every Amish school will be."

By early afternoon, the day had become hot enough that Lillian opened a window near her desk. A gust of breeze blew in and carried the arid smell of smoke into the schoolroom. Lillian looked up from the paper she was grading and glanced outside. A large cornfield stood across the road from the school. The tall pale tan stalks hadn't yet been harvested and their dry leaves crackled in the brisk wind. She saw a thin column of smoke rising from the far end of the field near the river.

Frowning, she rose from her chair and moved toward the front door. Had Mr. Hanson decided to burn his trash today? The country was under an open burning ban because of the drought, but not everyone complied with the rule.

On the porch, Lillian shaded her eyes and looked south. Mr. Hanson's cornfield curved around the building on three sides like a wide horseshoe. A swirl of wind picked up fallen leaves from beneath the trees by the road and added them to the large pile that had accumulated beside the porch. Unease crept up Lillian's spine.

The school, situated on a small hillock, was backed by a taller rise with a thick stand of woods that ended in a sheer bluff above the river. To the north, a high wooded ridge separated the school from the collection of farms beyond that were also located inside the bend of the river. The road in front of the school made a loop through the area that was mainly Amish farms. The covered bridge at Bowmans Crossing was the only way in and out.

Susan came outside and stood beside Lillian. "Do you smell smoke?"

"It's coming from Mr. Hanson's farmstead."

"Surely he can see the wind is too strong and in the wrong direction for burning today."

A huge explosion rocked the quiet afternoon, startling Lillian and making Susan shriek. Flames and black smoke shot skyward from the Hansons' farm. Lillian watched in shock as flaming debris flew high into the air.

Susan gripped Lillian's arm. "What was that?"

"I'm not sure. Perhaps a gasoline tank." The noise of excited children's voices rose inside the school.

"Should I run to the phone shack and call 9-1-1?" Susan asked, poised to dash away. The community telephone booth was a hundred yards down the road. A car went speeding past the school. Lillian recognized it as the one that belonged to Davey Mast. Was he headed for the phone booth to call for help? She had no way of knowing.

"Miss Merrick has a cell phone. We'll use that."

Lillian hurried Susan back inside. "Remain in your seats, children. There has been an explosion at the Hanson Farm across the way. Miss Merrick, would you be kind enough to notify 9-1-1? I want to make sure help is on the way."

"Of course." She pulled out her cell phone.

A gust of wind-driven smoke billowed in through the open window. Several children started coughing. Lillian motioned to Gabriel. "Shut the window, please."

Debra Merrick came over with the phone in her hand. "The local fire department has been alerted."

Was Timothy on call today? Even if he wasn't, he was sure to be among the people who would rush to help the Hansons.

Abe and Gabriel were at the windows looking out. Gabriel turned to her. "Should we go see if we can help?"

It wasn't a bad suggestion. Lillian chewed her lower lip. Perhaps she should send several of the older boys.

"Teacher. The fire is coming this way." The fear in Abe's voice drew her quickly to the window.

A wall of flames spewing dense smoke was spreading into the cornfield. The broad tongues of fire bent low and surged forward with each gust of the wind. Behind it, she could see the fire had spread into the trees along the river near the bridge. The only thing between the school and the flames was a narrow road. Would the fire be able to jump it? There wasn't much fuel for the blaze in their short lawn, but the building itself was wooden. There was plenty of fuel in the woods behind the school. Would they be safe here? Even as the question crossed her mind, a burning leaf of corn spiraled down from the sky and landed in the center of the road.

No. They weren't safe. The wind was too strong.

"We could go through the woods behind the school and down to the river," Gabriel suggested.

Lillian assessed the possible escape routes. The hill was steep and densely wooded terrain. Getting up and over it and down to the river would take time. "The fire is already spreading through the woods along the river. With so much wind, it could get in front of us. I don't think we should chance it. The young ones won't be able to move fast enough."

Debra moved to stand beside Lillian. "I can take some of the children in my car and drive out of here."

Lillian considered the idea. The sun was almost blotted out by the dense billowing clouds of smoke, but it was easy to see the wall of flames growing closer. Even with the windows closed, the smell of smoke was overwhelming.

"The only way out of this area is back across the bridge. The road only leads to other farms and it curves back and forth in the woods as it goes over the ridge. You might become trapped. *Nee*, I will keep all the children here. You are free to go if you wish."

"I'm staying with you and the kids."

"Danki."

Lillian turned to the class and spoke in Pennsylvania *Deitsch* so they could all understand her. "Children, you must listen to me very carefully and do what I say without question. There is a fire heading this way. I want you seventh- and eighth-grade boys to wet your handkerchiefs from the water can. Use them to cover your noses and mouths. If you don't have one, borrow one. Get whatever you can find that will hold water and start throwing it on the school building outside. Use the water from the horse tank and make a bucket brigade from the pump. Wet the roof as well as you can. Soak the area around our propane tank, too. Be quick and come back inside when I ring the bell. Each of you choose a partner and don't get separated from that person. Gabriel, you're in charge. Go."

Eight boys scrambled to her desk for water and were soon out the door. She turned to the remaining children and prayed she was making the right decision. "I want the rest of you to file down quietly into the basement. Each student in the older grades will take the hand of one younger child and lead everyone downstairs. Susan, take them all into the coal cellar and check to see that you can open the outside doors. They haven't been used in years."

The school board had taken out the coal stove and installed a new propane furnace four years earlier, but the coal storage area remained. The cavelike structure jutted out from the side of the basement, so the building wasn't directly over it. It had a thick wooden door they could close off to the basement. The curved walls and roof of the cellar were hand-hewn stone and covered with earth. It was fireproof. They could escape through the outside chute doors if the school building caught fire.

Lillian turned to Debra. "Go with Susan. You'll be safe underground. Use your phone to tell the fire department what we're doing first, then help Susan keep the children calm."

"Are you sure this is wise?" Debra stared at her with wide fear-filled eyes.

"The firefighters will make getting here a priority," she said with absolute confidence. The closest fire station was across the river about a mile from Bowmans Crossing. One covered wooden bridge stood between them. Had the fire reached it already? Were they cut off? Only God knew, but Timothy and the Bowman family would move heaven and earth to save the children even if they had to swim the river. Of that she was certain. "Go downstairs, Debra. You'll be safe there."

"I hope you're right about this." Debra sprinted for the staircase leading to the basement.

Lillian untied her apron as she hurried to her desk. After wetting the material, she tied it around her face. At the front door, she paused and closed her eyes. "Dear Lord, let this be the right decision. Save these children and protect the men coming to help us."

Protect Timothy. Why did I let him leave in anger yesterday? Forgive me, Timothy.

Taking a deep breath, she pulled open the door and

went out to ring the bell. She made sure she had all the boys as they raced inside. When they were safe, she said, "Get down to the basement."

Susan came up the steps just as Lillian reached it. "Teacher, I can't get the outside doors open."

"I'll go around to the back and see if something is blocking it." Gabriel started for the door.

Lillian grabbed his arm. "*Nee*, get downstairs with the others. I'll go."

When he did as she told him, Lillian pulled her wet apron over her face again and stepped out into the dense smoke.

Chapter Five

The sound of an explosion had pulled Timothy, his brothers and the rest of the men working in the Bowman furniture shop outside. Timothy stared toward the bridge and saw dense smoke billowing above the trees on the north side of the river. It was impossible to tell how far away the explosion had been, but he thought it had to have been from the Hanson Farm.

Timothy's mother came out of the house and stood on the steps, her eyes wide with fright. "What was that? Is anyone hurt?"

"It wasn't here," Isaac, Timothy's father yelled across to his wife. "It came from over the river."

Timothy's pager started beeping. Noah's pager went off next.

"What do you think that was? Should we head over there?" Noah asked as he silenced his pager.

"Nee," Isaac said. "You should go with your fire crew. They will be here soon. Everyone else, come with me. Grab shovels, anything that you can use to beat out the flames. We must protect the bridge. Samuel, go to the house and have your mother give us all the towels and

blankets she can spare. If we soak them, we can use them to beat out the flames. Luke, bring every fire extinguisher from the shop." The men all ran to accomplish their tasks and were soon headed toward the footbridge.

Timothy and Noah ran up the lane toward the highway. As soon as they reached the road, a black pickup driven by their English neighbor and fireman, Walter Osborne, skidded to a halt on the pavement. Part of Walter's job was to collect the Amish volunteers and get them to the fire station as quickly as possible. He rolled down the window and shouted, "Get in. Hurry."

"What was it?" Timothy asked as he and Noah climbed into the backseat.

"We aren't sure. The call came from a woman at the school. Some kind of public health worker. All she knew was that the explosion came from the Hanson Farm. The field across from the school is on fire, and the flames are heading toward them."

Walter stepped on the gas. "I've got one more to pick up."

"Who?" Noah asked.

"John Miller." The burly local blacksmith and farrier lived a little more than a mile away.

"Did they evacuate the school?" Timothy asked, meeting Noah's worried gaze.

Walter sent the truck rocketing down the road. "No, the fire has them cut off. The teacher decided it was safer to put the kids in a cold room. You two went to that school. What kind of cold room does it have?"

Perplexed, Timothy glanced again at Noah. His brother shrugged. Suddenly, Timothy realized what the caller might have meant. "Not a cold room, the coal room. It's a cavelike area off to the north side of the school basement. The teacher there, Lillian Keim, is one of the smartest women I know. If anyone can keep the children safe, she can."

He prayed for all the children in peril and for her. He'd been foolish to let a misunderstanding jeopardize their friendship. He wasn't sure he could face himself knowing his last words to her were the ones he'd spoken in anger.

John was standing by his mailbox at the end of his lane. He still wore his big leather apron over his clothes. He didn't bother opening the door of the truck, but vaulted into the bed and pounded on the roof to let Walter know he was on board.

Walter hit the gas again. In a few minutes, they reached a white steel building that sat by itself on a plot of land just off the highway. The wail of a siren blared from a speaker on the roof as one of the two metal garage doors rose. The main fire engine pulled out just as a second pickup loaded with volunteers turned into the parking lot. The men, all Amish farmers and their non-Amish driver, piled out, grabbed their gear and quickly jumped onto the engine. There was none of the usual chatter today. Many of the men had children or grandchildren at the school.

As the others pulled away, Timothy and Noah entered the building and donned their fire gear. The coats, pants and hats were heavy, but if they had to enter a burning building, their fireproof gear would be needed along with their air packs.

The men quickly settled themselves in the station's smaller fire truck and pulled out of the building with Walter in the driver's seat. As they sped down the road toward the river, Timothy saw dozens of men and boys, some in wagons and some on foot and horseback, heading in the same direction.

The first fire truck had been stopped just past the covered bridge by a wall of flames. A burning tree blocked the road, and the woods on either side were heavily involved. Through the dense smoke, Timothy could make out the farmhouse with flames licking out from under the roof. This was a bad one.

Timothy's radio crackled and he heard the fire chief's voice. "Truck Two, get your hoses on that tree. We've got to get it out of our way."

Noah and Timothy leaped off the vehicle to comply. As they unreeled a line, Timothy found himself working side by side with men in fire gear and men in straw hats and suspenders. Every fire call he'd been involved with was the same. Neighbors rushed in to help each other.

With the line stretched, Timothy braced for the pressure surge as the water filled the hose. More men grabbed on behind him, and within a few moments he had a wide spray of water soaking the roadblock. The blaze was quickly extinguished. Timothy dialed back the pressure and kept a light spray covering the two men who rushed forward with chain saws. Someone produced a log chain. The downed tree was hooked to the main fire truck and quickly pulled aside.

The fire commander came up calling orders. "Truck One, get your crew up to the farmhouse. We have injuries there. Truck Two, get to the school. We have a tanker coming from Berlin, but they're twenty minutes out. This road is the only way in and there are ten farms past this point. I've called for aircraft support and we have a chopper coming."

"In this wind?" Walter asked in amazement.

"They know we have a school full of children out there, and the crew is willing to risk it. Let's pray they can get a dump on the school before it's too late."

They couldn't be too late. Timothy had to believe that Lillian and the children were safe.

He jumped back on board the engine. Their smaller vehicle held only five hundred gallons of water. The larger truck held a thousand gallons. Without fire hydrants to hook up to in rural areas, the only water available was what the trucks carried. Timothy looked at the blaze leaping from treetop to treetop and roaring through the cornfield in front of them. They were definitely going to need more water.

Thick smoke made Lillian's eyes water so badly she could barely see the heavy-gauge wire wrapped around the coal chute door handles. The stiff wire had been turned tightly and it refused to unwind. A burning corn leaf swirled in and landed on her arm, scorching her sleeve. She beat out the ember with her palm, but it left a charred hole in her dress.

The roar and crackle of the approaching fire was so loud she wanted to put her hands over her ears and hide. How could this be happening?

She glanced up into the roiling ember-filled smoke sweeping over everything. The firestorm would soon be past, but that didn't mean the building would be spared. The children were safe where they were, but they had to have an escape route if the school caught fire and they couldn't get out that way.

She bent with renewed determination and finally freed the wire, throwing it aside. She noticed blood on her hands, but she didn't take time to look for her injury.

Another blazing ember landed on her arm. She shook it off, stomping it out with her shoe as it started to spread through the grass at her feet. Looking around, she saw several other small fires in the grass. It was then she noticed the barn roof was already on fire. Flames were licking at the front of Debra's car from a cedar bush beside it.

Lillian grabbed the handle of one iron door. She needed to get under cover and out of the smoke. Although the wire was off the handles, the door wouldn't budge. She tried the other one without success. The smoke was choking her even through the cloth over her face. She grew light-headed. Fear and frustration tore a cry of anguish from her throat as she looked to the heavens. "Please, Lord, give me strength."

Walter drove into the dense smoke as quickly as he dared. Noah kept an eye on the right edge of the road while Timothy kept an eye on the left side and they were able to help guide him along. Once they passed out of the woods, the going was easier. The corn, while providing plenty of fuel for the fire, had burned off quickly, leaving only charred smoldering stubble in the field. Embers danced around them in the air. As they drew close to the school, Timothy could see a wall of flames in front of them being pushed by the wind.

"We've got to get in front of this," Walter said through gritted teeth.

Timothy tried to judge how far they were from the school, but he couldn't make out the building through the smoke. "The fire's speed may work in our favor."

"How?" Noah asked.

Walter swung the truck away from a blazing cedar at the edge of the road. "The fire can go around the school so quickly that the structure may not catch fire. A lot of buildings are lost to smoldering embers that ignite after the main fire has passed."

A gust of wind opened a break in the smoke. Timothy caught sight of the school. It was still standing. But for how long?

Please, Lord, keep them safe. Have mercy on the children. On Lillian.

Walter maneuvered the fire truck onto the front lawn of the school. The far end of the front porch was already burning. Noah, Timothy and John were out of the vehicle a second later and pulling the hose into position to soak the main building. Timothy saw that the small stable behind the school was already engulfed in flames. A blazing car sat beside it, but there was nothing they could do. They didn't have enough water. The heavy smoke made visibility almost nil as the wind whipped burning embers all around them.

Once they had a steady stream of water pouring onto the front of the school, Walter tapped Timothy on the shoulder. "Check inside. We don't have much water left."

Sprinting up the steps, he raced inside. The room was empty as he had expected, but he shouted for Lillian at the top of his lungs. He didn't get a reply. The stairs to the basement were at the rear of the building. The wooden steps were old and steep. In the pitch-black cellar, he turned on his lantern and shouted again. This time, he heard voices answering him.

He pulled open the coal room door. "Is everyone okay?"

Several dozen frightened faces stared back at him from the gloom. Lillian wasn't among them. His heart dropped like a rock. "Where's your teacher? Where's Lillian?"

Chapter Six

❧

Timothy moved into the group of children and saw Susan Yoder sitting beside Debra on the floor. She pointed to the back of the room. "Lillian is outside trying to open the doors."

Timothy waded through the rest of the children to reach the back of the coal cellar. His torch illuminated the rungs of an iron ladder set into the stone wall. Overhead, a pair of rusty iron doors remained closed, but he could see light coming in around them. "Lillian, are you there?"

"I'm here." Her muffled voice came from above. "There was a piece of wire around the handles. I got it off, but I still can't lift the door. I think the hinges are rusted shut." A coughing fit followed her words.

He pushed against the door, but it wouldn't budge. Smoke swirled in through the opening. The crackle of the fire outside grew steadily louder.

He grabbed his radio mike. "Can someone get around back and help Lillian pry open the cellar doors on the north side of the building?"

"No can do at the moment," Walter's breathless voice

crackled over the radio. "The porch is on fire and we're out of water. Stay put if you and the kids are safe. Captain says the chopper is on its way."

Without water, all the men had to smother the fire with was the dirt they could dig and shovel on it. He glanced at the children gathered around him. "We're okay. Get Lillian to safety if it gets too close."

Timothy stepped up and wedged his shoulder against the door. If the school went up in flames, this would be the only way out. He shoved and it creaked open a bare inch. Abe and Gabriel came in with a couple of chairs, stood on them and reaching up added their strength to the task. It wasn't enough.

Then suddenly, the old door gave a groan and swung upward. Timothy saw Lillian looking down at him, and his heart started beating again. She was covered in soot but unharmed. He'd never been so glad to see anyone. Beside her stood John Miller. Timothy knew he had the blacksmith's strength to thank for getting the door open.

"Lillian, are you okay?" Timothy asked.

"*Ja*, I'm fine." She started down the ladder.

He climbed down and waited until she reached the floor beside him. Then he pulled her into his arms and hugged her tight. She was safe and it felt so right to hold her in his arms. "I didn't know what to think when I didn't see you with the children."

His radio crackled to life. "We have to pull back. The chopper is here. Prepare for a water dump," Walter shouted.

John shut the doors, plunging them into darkness. Timothy reluctantly let go of Lillian, fighting the urge to gather her into his arms and hold her close again. This wasn't the time or the place.

She took a step back, but her fingers caressed his cheek before she crossed her arms and dropped her gaze to the floor. Something was different between them. He forced his mind back to the crisis at hand. "Are all the children here?"

"*Ja*, they are all here."

He faced her students. "A helicopter is coming to dump a big bucket of water over the school. It's going to make a lot of noise, but we are safe in here. Your teacher picked the best possible place for you."

Lillian gave him a weak smile. He clicked on his radio. "Go ahead."

As soon as he spoke, the sound of the rotor blades roared in overhead. The building trembled in the force of the downdraft, sending dust drifting down from the basement ceiling. A loud swoosh was followed by the sound of water hammering onto the roof. Some gushed in through the old coal chute, soaking the stones at the back of the cave. Less than a minute later, the sound of the helicopter faded into the distance.

Noah came down the basement stairs, his helmet lantern casting a bright arc of light before him. "Is everyone all right?"

Timothy stepped out of the cave and slapped a hand on his brother's shoulder. "We're fine."

Susan stood up. "We have one injury. Debra twisted her ankle coming down the stairs."

"It's not serious. Take care of the children," Debra said from her place on the floor.

"Where's Hannah?" Noah looked over the crowd of children pressing close.

"I'm right here, *Onkel* Noah."

"They are all present and accounted for," Lillian assured him.

Noah's worried face relaxed. "The captain will let a convoy of vehicles in to collect the *kinder* as soon as the tanker from Berlin can put out any spot fires between us and the bridge. *Daed* told him everyone is welcome to go to our house."

"Is it safe for us to stay here?" Lillian asked.

"I think so," Noah said. "The fire has moved on."

"Then I'm staying here with the children until their parents come to collect them or it is safe to let them go home."

Walter came to the top of the stairs. "We have to go, guys. The tanker has set up the portable pond just up the road. We need to refill and get up to the ridge."

As much as Timothy wanted to stay with Lillian and the children, he still had a job to do. There were people, homes, livestock and crops still in danger. He knelt beside Debra. "Can you walk?"

"No, I don't think so."

Noah stepped up beside her. "Let's get you out of this dark cellar so we can take a proper look at your ankle." He lifted her in his arms.

The movement brought tears to her eyes. "How am I going to drive my car like this?"

Noah hesitated, but said, "The fire got your car."

She looked up with wide shocked eyes. "Are you serious?"

He nodded. "I'm afraid so."

"What am I going to do?"

Lillian patted her shoulder. "You're welcome to stay with me until you can sort it out. I'm sure we can find a driver to take you home if you don't have someone who can come and get you."

Timothy knew Lillian well enough to hear the slight hesitation in her voice. Her family wasn't as open to outsiders as his was. Plus, her family's farm was in the path of the fire on the other side of the ridge. She might not have a home to go to tonight. He followed as Noah carried Debra up the stairs, taking care not to jostle her more than necessary. Once he reached the schoolroom, Lillian stepped around him and pulled her chair away from the desk. He placed Debra gently in it.

Lillian turned over the wastebasket, pulled a sweater from the bottom drawer of her desk and folded it for Debra to elevate her foot on.

"*Danki*, Lillian." Noah gently raised Debra's leg. The ankle was swollen and turning dark. He gave her a half-hearted smile. "Nurse, what is your professional opinion? Do you need a doctor? I can call for an ambulance, but it may take a while."

She gently felt the sides and top of her foot. "I think it's just a bad sprain. Ice it, wrap it snugly and keep it elevated would be my professional advice. Leave the ambulance free for someone who truly needs it."

"As you wish. I know Lillian will take good care of you." Noah rose to his feet and headed for the door.

Lillian caught Timothy by the arm. "God go with you and be careful not to make His job more difficult."

He covered her hand with his own, willing her to understand how much her words meant to him. "I'll be careful, and I'm sorry. I hope you know that."

Lillian smiled tenderly. "Not as sorry as I am. Are we friends again?"

"Always," he whispered. His eyes darkened as he

gazed into hers. His grip on her hand tightened, sending her pulse soaring.

Her racing heart was surely due to her close call with the fire and not to the simple touch of his hand. She stared into his eyes and saw deep affection in their depths. Was it only friendship, or something more? She looked away first.

They had both suffered a fright. It was only natural that it made her more attuned to him. She tried to get her jumbled emotions under control and put their relationship back on the proper path. Pulling her hand away, she took a step back. "*Goot.* Now go. Others need you."

"Keep an eye out for any hot spots that might flare up around the building."

"We will."

He nodded once and then hurried out the door. She listened to the sound of his fire engine as it faded in the distance, and swallowed back her tears. Their friendship was mended and he was in God's hands. She couldn't ask for more. She turned her attention to the children gathered at the windows looking out at the charred field and the towering smoke.

Susan looked at Lillian with tears in her eyes. "I can see Mr. Hanson's house is burning. I hope everyone is okay."

"We can pray for them."

"We should do something more. Can we take up a collection for them?" Susan asked hopefully. The Hansons were not members of their Amish community, but they were neighbors in need.

"Of course. When we come back to school on Monday, we will put together a gift basket for them." Lillian knew they might not hold classes on Monday, but she wanted to reassure the children that things would return to normal as soon as possible.

Debra adjusted her foot with a grimace. "I'm sorry to be so much trouble."

"You're not trouble. I need help getting the word out that the children are safe. You have a phone."

Lillian opened the top drawer of her desk. She took out a sheet of paper and handed it to Debra. "Here are some emergency contact phone numbers. They are our local telephone booths, some English neighbors of the children and several local businesses. Leave a message and your number if you get an answering machine."

"It's the least I can do." Debra took the paper from her.

Lillian went to the front of the school and looked out at the porch. The steps and railing were charred, but most of the damage looked superficial. Her barn and Debra's car beside it were little more than smoldering heaps of junk. Shading her eyes, she tried to pick Timothy out from among the firemen strung across the field and woods, but she couldn't tell one from the other.

Three fire engines were parked along the road. One, a tanker truck, was dumping water into a large square yellow holding tank. When the tanker was empty, it made a U-turn and headed back toward the river. A smaller engine crew dropped a fat hose into the tank. A few minutes later, the men pulled it out, jumped back on board their truck and sped toward the fire. A white SUV with the sheriff's logo on the door stopped on the road. She recognized the officer who got out as Sheriff Nick Bradley. "Is Hannah okay?"

Hannah's mother was Sheriff Bradley's adopted daughter. The little girl ran out onto the porch steps and waved. "I'm fine, Papa Nick."

"Stay with your teacher until your mother gets here," he shouted, and got back into his vehicle. A second later, he took off toward the blaze.

A column of dense black smoke boiled into the sky as tongues of orange flames leaped along the base that stretched the width of the field. It was moving away from the school toward a heavily wooded ridge with frightening speed. Beyond the ridge were ten more farms, Amish and English, including her home. She prayed for the safety of her brother and sister and for the men risking their lives to stop the wildfire.

As she turned to go back inside, she noticed a wisp of smoke rising from beneath the lowest step of the porch. Timothy had told her to watch out for hot spots. She went back into the building. "Abe, bring the fire extinguishers and come with me. I want the first, second and third grades to stay inside with Susan until someone from your family arrives. The rest of you come outside and help me put out any smoldering spots."

The next hour was busy for Lillian. The Bowman women from across the river were the first ones to arrive. Ana Bowman, Rebecca, Samuel's wife, and Hannah's mother, Mary, climbed down from their buggy. Mary scooped Hannah into a fierce hug. Ana watched them with her hands pressed to her chest. "We give praise to the Lord this day. He has kept all our children safe."

Rebecca carried a large quilted bag slung over her shoulder. She placed her free arm around Lillian's shoulders. "I'm so glad you are unharmed. One of the firemen told us your visiting nurse was injured. Where is she?"

Before her marriage to Samuel Bowman, Rebecca had been a lay nurse in the community. She had plenty of experience treating sprains, burns, assorted injuries and illnesses. Lillian pointed toward the school. "She is inside. Her name is Debra Merrick."

"I'll see what I can do for her. It appears they may have the fire under control."

Lillian turned to look north. While there was still smoke rising, it wasn't as dense, and it didn't seem to be moving. She noticed only a few flickering patches of orange flames at the far end of the charred field. "God be praised."

Ana and Mary took Hannah home in the buggy while Rebecca remained with Lillian. By ones and twos, more mothers made their way to the school to collect their children. A half hour later, Lillian saw one of the fire trucks was making its way slowly back. It stopped in front of the school. Silas Mast, the school board president, climbed down along with Joshua and Timothy. Lillian's heart skipped a beat at the sight of Timothy's soot-covered face. He gave her a brief nod before walking around the back of the school. The truck drove on. Carl ran out to meet his father. Abe followed more slowly.

Silas knelt to put his arms around his youngest. "Are you boys all right?"

"It was a mighty exciting day at school, *Daed*," Carl said with a big grin. "Was it fun to ride on the fire truck? I want to do that someday."

"It wasn't as much fun as you might think." Silas rose and spoke to Lillian. "I will take them home now, for I know their mother is worried. Do you need any help here?"

"Not at the moment. We have some smoke damage inside, but I see no reason why we can't reopen the school after things are cleaned. It shouldn't take more than half a day. Joshua, Hannah has already gone home with Mary."

The tension eased on Joshua's sweat- and smoke-stained face. "My wife is a *goot* mother. You have my thanks for keeping the *kinder* safe."

"And my thanks, as well," Silas said. "I will come tomorrow and inspect the building to see what repairs are needed." Taking his boys by the hand, he began walking toward his farm on the far side of the ridge.

Timothy came around to the front of the building. "I don't see any problem spots."

Lillian resisted the urge to gently wipe the grime from his tired face. "My students have been diligently putting out any smoldering places."

Timothy nodded. "I think the danger of flare-ups here has passed, but someone should keep an eye on that car until we can get some flame-retardant to spray on it."

Lillian scanned the charred field. "I can't believe you got the blaze stopped before it reached the forest on the ridge."

Timothy rubbed his eyes with his knuckles. "The water drops by the helicopter helped, but we wouldn't have been able to stop it if Davey Mast hadn't had the presence of mind and the courage to cut a firebreak between the burning field and the woods. He saw what was happening and raced to get a tractor and plow from his employer's farm."

"He may have saved every farm beyond the ridge, including his father's," Joshua said.

"I saw his car go past shortly after the explosion, and I wondered why he was driving so fast. Many will be grateful for his quick thinking. Perhaps this will lead to a reconciliation of their family." Lillian was surprised that Silas hadn't mentioned his oldest son's deed to her or the boys.

"I pray you are right, but Silas wouldn't speak to him today," Timothy said.

Silas wasn't forbidden to speak to his son by the rules of shunning. Baptized members of the Amish church couldn't eat at the same table with him, do business with him, accept anything from his hand or ride in his car. Thanking the boy for his quick thinking and courage was certainly permitted.

"Is Rebecca here?" Joshua asked.

"She is inside with the visiting nurse."

"Two nurses, that's great. We have several fellows with minor burns, including my reckless brother. I'll send them here."

She turned to Timothy in alarm. "Are you hurt?"

He shook his head. "I'm the cautious one. Noah is the fellow who rushes in where wiser men fear to go, and this time he paid a small price. Hopefully, it will teach him a lesson."

Lillian pressed a hand to her suddenly tight chest. Drawing a deep breath, she waited until the painful hammering of her heart slowed. She was being foolish. Timothy wasn't hurt. She could see that with her own eyes. "Bring anyone injured here. I will let Rebecca and Debra know they are coming. I have first aid supplies on hand, and I know Rebecca will have brought some with her."

He nodded. "We'll let them know." The two men headed back across the burned field. A short time later, she saw Timothy driving a wagon toward the school. Noah and two other men sat in the bed of the wagon. After pulling to a stop beside her, the men got out and went into the school building all under their own power. Noah was the only one limping heavily.

Lillian stood beside the wagon gazing up at Timothy. "You look worn out."

A half smile lifted the corner of his mouth. "Add hot and dirty to that description, and you'll have me in a nutshell. I may jump in the river on my way home."

At least he could joke about it. "Was it as bad as it looked from here?"

"It was. Do you need anything?"

"We're fine. Most of the children have been picked up already. Was anyone hurt at the Hanson Farm?"

"I heard Mr. Hanson suffered some serious injuries in the explosion. His wife passed out from the smoke in the house, but one of the firemen was able to get her out in time. They have both been taken to the hospital. I'm afraid their home is a total loss."

"How sad. Has anyone notified the family?"

"Sheriff Bradley said they notified a son who lives in Berlin."

"Have you heard how the fire started?"

"I haven't, but the men are saying it looks suspicious. I'm sure our fire chief will get to the bottom of it as soon as he can." Timothy licked his chapped lips and grimaced.

"Let me get you some water. You must be thirsty."

"I am, but I can get my own drink." He jumped down from the wagon and stumbled slightly. She put out a hand against his chest to steady him. A jolt of awareness surged up her arm and sent heat rising into her cheeks. She'd never had this reaction to Timothy before. What was wrong with her today?

Chapter Seven

Timothy looked down at Lillian's small hand pressed against his chest. The delicate hand of a capable woman. He covered her fingers with his own and wondered at the rush of emotion clogging his throat. He was a blessed man to have such a dear friend.

She pulled away from him. "You look ready to fall over, and Rebecca doesn't need another patient. Wait here, and I'll get you some water."

"Bossy, bossy, bossy. Just like the dog in the book." He winked, and she gave him a timid smile.

"It comes from being a teacher. I tell children what to do and I expect them to do it."

He leaned against the wagon wheel and sighed. He was bone-tired. "I shall be a good pupil and do as the teacher says."

"That kind of attitude will move you to the head of the class."

"I'm not at the head of your class already?"

"*Nee*, you are not. I consider you more of a problem child. You have plenty of room for improvement."

He laughed out loud. "I pity the fellows who come

looking to court you. I can imagine you handing out grade cards on their performance as suitors."

Her chin came up. "None have risen above a C-plus. Alas, now you know why I'm still unwed."

It was good to be teased by her and to respond in kind. This was the way their friendship had been for ages. He began to see how rare and special their relationship was, and he cherished it even more. "I'm glad none have made a better grade in your eyes."

She tipped her head to the side. A strange look entered her eyes. "Are you? Why?"

He almost blurted out that he was glad she didn't find anyone else attractive enough to court, because he wished to court her.

Where had that thought come from? The idea was as frightening as the fire had been.

He managed to say, "For the children's sake. You are a fine teacher, and they need you."

For a moment, he thought she looked disappointed, but she quickly smiled. "I do love my job. I can't imagine meeting someone who could make me want to give it up. I'll be right back with that drink. Should I send water out to the other men, too?"

"That would be great." As she walked away, he let out a breath he hadn't realized he was holding.

Courting Lillian was a ridiculous idea, wasn't it? They were friends and had been for years. Yet something had changed today. After fearing for her life and then holding her safe in his arms, he realized his feelings for her had gone beyond those of a friend.

What, if anything, should he do about it?

If he did ask her to walk out with him, what would she say? She was likely to tell him no. And then what? How could they return to a simple friendship after that? And what if she said yes? Where would that lead?

Lillian returned with a large pail of water, a ladle and several plastic cups. "This is the best I could do."

"It's fine."

Her warm smile and her bright eyes gazing at him made it hard to think straight. He needed to put some distance between them before he said or did something stupid. Like kiss her. She had the most kissable-looking lips. Why hadn't he noticed that before?

He was definitely suffering from some kind of shock.

Taking the water and supplies from her, he put them in the back of the wagon. Then he climbed onto the seat, picked up the reins and put the horses in motion. He glanced over his shoulder to see her watching him with a worried expression on her face. He was overwhelmed with the need to go back and comfort her, but he didn't give in to that desire. Instead, he pushed the horses to a faster trot until they rounded the bend in the road and left the school behind.

If only his mixed up emotions were as easy to outdistance.

Lillian frowned as she watched Timothy drive away. Something about his abrupt departure didn't feel right. It was as if he were running away from her.

Sighing, she dismissed the notion. He needed to get back to his fellow firefighters, and she was reading too much into his behavior. It had been a trying day for everyone. Over the next half hour, she saw many of the volunteers returning home. A few of the men stopped to pick up their children. She kept watching the activity on the road, but she didn't see the Bowman brothers leave.

A short time later, she saw her brother coming across the field toward the school. She wasn't surprised to see him. He would've seen the smoke and come to investigate. He was riding bareback on Goldie, the little Haflinger mare who normally pulled their pony cart. He hadn't wasted time harnessing her.

Lillian waited until he drew close. "I am well, *bruder*."

"I'm right pleased to see that. Looks like it might have been a near thing."

She glanced around at the blackened grass, burned-out barn and heavily damaged porch. "It was. We were truly blessed that it wasn't any worse."

"Whose car is that?" he asked, staring at the charred wreck that was still smoking.

"It belongs to the visiting nurse."

"I hope she wasn't in it."

"*Nee*. She was inside with us, but she is stranded here until tomorrow. Where is Amanda?"

"I left her with Granny Weaver." The elderly woman wasn't related to Lillian's family, but everyone in the area called her Granny. She lived with her son, and daughter-in-law on a farm a half mile down the road from Lillian's house.

Jeremiah waved a hand toward the charred cornfield. "Old man Hanson should have let me harvest his crop last week. I offered to do it for a fair price and he practically threw me off the place. Shouted at me like I was some kind of thief. Now he's left with nothing, and it serves him right."

"We must not take delight in another man's misfortune. He and his wife were injured."

His eyes filled with remorse. "I didn't know that. Were they badly hurt?"

"Timothy said they were both taken to the hospital. Have you seen him out there?"

"I saw all the Bowman brothers and Isaac, too. Why?"

"Most of the men have left, but I haven't seen Timothy leave yet."

"I'm sure some of the firemen will be watching for flare-ups for the next few hours. Have all the *kinder* gone home?"

"Sophie Hochstetler is still here. She is inside with the nurse. Once her father comes, I will be free to go."

"I saw Wayne helping roll up the hoses with the firemen. He should be along soon."

"There is something more I must tell you. I have invited Debra to stay the night with us."

"Who would that be? One of the children?"

"The owner of that burned-out car."

A quick frown creased his brow. "An *Englischer*? You should not have done that. You know our *daed* would object. We should not mix with outsiders."

"She is a person in need. I could not turn my back on her. Besides, you are hardly in a position to lecture me, *bruder*. I saw you riding in a car with Davey Mast, and he is shunned. What would *Daed* say to that?"

Jeremiah's lips pressed into a tight thin line, but he made no further comment. Lillian didn't expect that he would. "Debra has a badly turned ankle. Her brother will be here first thing tomorrow to take her home. Come and meet her."

"If I must." Jeremiah slid off his horse and followed Lillian to the school. Inside, she introduced him to Debra. The poor woman looked deathly pale, and she had dark circles of pain under her eyes.

Sophie, one of Lillian's first-grade students, was seated

at her desk nearby. The petite blonde girl looked up shyly and spoke in *Deitsch*. "Can I go now? I don't like this lady."

Sophie rarely liked anyone other than her father, but she tolerated her teacher. Lillian nodded. "Your father will be here soon. You can wait for him outside."

The child scampered out the door. Debra gave Jeremiah a weak smile. "Your sister was kind enough to offer to put me up for the night. I hope that's all right. I can surely find somewhere else to stay if it's an imposition."

"Its fine," Jeremiah managed to say in spite of his clenched jaw. "Can you ride a horse bareback?"

Debra's smile vanished and her eyes widened. "I've never been on a horse. I'm not sure today is the best day for my first lesson."

Lillian patted Debra's hand. "Goldie is not a big horse, and she is as tame as they come."

Debra still looked uncertain. "I'm always saying I like to learn new things. I guess I'd better prove it."

"That's the spirit." Lillian slipped her arm around Debra and helped her to her feet. Between Lillian and Jeremiah, they managed to get her outside and onto the docile mare. Wayne Hochstetler arrived to take Sophie with him, so Lillian was able to leave with Debra and Jeremiah. As she walked beside Debra to steady her on the horse, she couldn't keep her gaze away from the firemen still working in the distance. Timothy was out there somewhere.

Now that the rush of emotions and fear had passed, she had time to examine her feelings more closely. Something had changed today. She had changed.

In her heart, she knew she would never forget how it felt to be held in Timothy's arms. And he must never know that.

Chapter Eight

The following morning, Timothy groaned when he realized he'd made another wrong cut in the board on the bench in front of him. It was his third mistake of the day, and it wasn't even nine o'clock. He wanted to blame his carelessness on being tired after firefighting the previous day, but he knew that wasn't his problem. His problem was Lillian. The way she had touched his cheek had almost been a caress. What did it mean?

"What's the matter?" Joshua asked when he finished drilling a hole in the block of wood he was working on.

"Nothing. Everything. Someone else needs to run this table saw, or we'll be out of good wood by noon." Timothy tossed aside the ruined piece.

"I can take over for you. It's not like you to make mistakes. Don't you feel well?"

Timothy glanced around the shop to see who else might overhear him. None of his other brothers were nearby. "You're married, Joshua. Can I ask you something?"

"Sure, but now you've really got me worried."

"When did you know you wanted to court Mary?

Were you worried she might not want to go out with you?"

"If I said I knew I wanted to court her the minute I laid eyes on her, I'd be lying. And of course, I was afraid she'd turn me down. Her father is the sheriff and I was fresh out of prison, remember?"

"For a crime you didn't commit," Timothy added quickly. Joshua had been wrongly imprisoned after he and Luke were picked up in a drug raid. Joshua had followed Luke to the city to try and convince their brother to give up drugs and return home. He'd spent six months in prison for being in the wrong place at the wrong time. It had been a difficult time for all the family, but in the end, God had shown them mercy. Luke was a reformed man and Joshua had married the love of his life.

Joshua folded his arms over his chest. "Are you planning to court someone?"

Timothy brushed the sawdust from the table. "I'm thinking about it."

"What's holding you back?"

"I'm afraid asking her out will ruin our friendship." It felt good to admit as much to Joshua. If he could talk about his feelings, maybe he could figure out what to do about them.

"Ah, you mean Lillian."

Timothy sent his brother a sidelong glance. "I reckon I shouldn't be surprised that her name sprang to mind."

Joshua laughed. "The two of you have been friends for ages. We all thought you would court her eventually. I'm surprised that you've waited this long. It's easy to see that she cares about you, so what's the problem?"

"She cares for me as a friend."

"Friendship is a fine place to start a courtship. It is a blessed man who calls his best friend his wife."

"It isn't that simple. If I ask her out and she says no, I'm afraid it will make things awkward between us. I don't want to lose Lillian's friendship. If I say nothing, we can stay friends."

"I understand your dilemma, but…can you remain her friend if you say nothing? Love is a hard emotion to hide. Do you love her?"

Timothy pondered his answer before he spoke. "I don't know. Maybe. I want to spend time with her. We have so much in common. I like to make her smile. I like the way I feel when she is near me. Is that love?"

"If you have to ask me that, then you aren't in love. Yet. What you have can grow into true love if that is God's will for the two of you, but many times a young man is simply infatuated with a woman. In love with the idea of being in love. Do you know what I mean?"

"How did *you* know when it was love?"

"I just did. I couldn't bear to be away from her. Look, why don't you ask Emma or Mary to broach the subject with Lillian? Lillian doesn't have to know the inquiry is coming from you."

But she would know. Timothy shook his head. "Forget I said anything. I'm happy being Lillian's friend, and I don't want to ruin that. It's foolish of me to think she might see me as anything else. I'm going to get another board."

"It doesn't sound to me like you're being completely honest with yourself. I still say send another woman to speak to her and see how she feels. Rebecca would do it."

"My wife will do what?" Samuel asked as he carried in a hand-carved headboard ready for sanding and propped it against the wall.

Timothy wasn't ready to share his feelings with his older brother. Joshua had no such reservations. "He wants to court Lillian, but he's afraid she'll say no and then they won't be friends anymore."

"And you want my wife to be your go-between? I don't see why not. It's a good idea."

"What is a good idea?" Noah asked from the open doorway of the workshop. Luke stood beside him.

Timothy stifled a groan. The last thing he wanted was to have all his brothers involved in this conversation.

Samuel slipped his thumbs under his suspenders. "Timothy is going to ask Rebecca to be his go-between with Lillian."

"I wondered when you two bookworms would get together," Luke said with a wink.

"We're not getting together in that way. I was considering the idea, but I'm sorry I brought it up. It wouldn't work. She loves teaching. She has often said she'll never give it up."

Samuel said, "She might feel that way now, but most women want families of their own eventually."

Was Samuel right? Timothy turned the idea over in his mind. Maybe all he needed to do was wait until she was ready to give up teaching. Then he wouldn't be asking her to choose between him and the job she loved. He could be patient.

But what if some other fellow caught her eye before he got up the nerve to ask her out? "Lillian isn't most women. Honestly, can we just forget I said anything?"

"Sure." Joshua exchanged a pointed look with Samuel. Timothy knew his brothers well enough to know they wouldn't let the subject rest. He shouldn't have said anything. He had been shaken up after fearing he'd lost her yesterday. A few days away from her would put everything back into perspective.

The sound of a car pulling to a stop in front of the workshop drew everyone's attention. "Who is it?" Samuel asked.

"It's our fire chief and the sheriff," Noah said from the doorway. "I think the state fire marshal is with them."

Timothy moved to look over Noah's shoulder. "That's him. I met him once at a training exercise."

Their father came out of the house and stood talking to the visitors beside their vehicle. After a few minutes, he turned to his sons and gestured for them to join him. When they reached his side, he spoke in *Deitsch*. "These men are investigating the fire at the Hanson Farm yesterday. They have evidence it was deliberately set. They would like to interview Lillian, her brother and the *Englisch* nurse. The sheriff would like one of us to go along."

"Why talk to Jeremiah? He wasn't at the school." Noah spoke quietly in *Deitsch*, too.

Isaac tipped his head toward the men. "They won't say."

Timothy exchanged a puzzled look with Noah, then spoke in English. "I'll go with you. Lillian's family won't readily speak to outsiders. They may be more comfortable talking to me."

Isaac nodded. "I will send your mother over, too. She is making up some things for the nurse."

As Timothy got in the car with the men, he realized he was thankful for any excuse to see Lillian again, even this one.

* * *

Lillian helped Debra hobble to the blue sofa in the living room. "Would you like a pillow to put your leg up on?"

"That would be great."

Lillian turned to Amanda. "Fetch the pillows from my bed and bring them here."

Amanda nodded and hurried away.

Debra sat down with a sigh. "You've taken wonderful care of me. I don't know how I can ever repay you."

"Repayment isn't necessary. We must do what we can for those in need."

"I'm grateful, I hope you know that. My brother should be here soon. He called when he left our apartment. I noticed that your brother wasn't at breakfast. Was that because of me?"

Amanda returned with a pillow, gave it to Lillian and rushed to the window. "There's a car coming."

"Perhaps that is your brother now." Lillian placed the pillows on the sofa and helped Debra get her foot settled comfortably, but she didn't answer Debra's question. Lillian didn't know where her brother was. He had been gone before she got up.

Amanda rushed to the screen door, eager to greet their visitors. "It's Timothy, sister. He is riding in an *Englisch* car."

"Then I had better go see what he wants. Amanda, stay with Debra, please."

Lillian struggled to hide the happy leap of her heart as Timothy approached the house. She schooled her features into what she hoped looked like mild curiosity. There were three men with him. She recognized his fire chief and Sheriff Bradley but not the other man.

"What brings you out this way, Timothy?" she asked, hoping her voice sounded normal.

He stopped at the front steps. "I came to check on you. You had quite a fright yesterday. Are you all right?"

She chuckled. "We all had quite a fright. I'm fine."

He nodded. "I should have known it would take more than a little smoke to rattle you."

"Don't let my calm teacher face fool you. I was scared out of my wits."

"I have to disagree. You kept your wits about you."

It pleased her that he thought well of her. "I'm sure you didn't come here to heap praise on my head. What can I do for you?"

His smile faded. He turned to the men who stood behind him. "Lillian, this is my fire chief, Eric Swanson. You know Sheriff Bradley, and this gentleman is Rodney George. Rodney is the state fire marshal. He'd like to speak to you. The fire yesterday wasn't an accident. It was deliberately set."

She stared at Mr. George in shock. "Who would do such a thing?"

Tall with a touch of gray at his temples, Rodney George seemed to be a man used to commanding others. "That is what I hope to find out. Is Miss Merrick still here?"

"*Ja*, Debra is inside."

"I'd like to ask the two of you some questions about yesterday?"

"I don't know what help we can be, but do come in." Lillian was curious to hear more details.

After everyone was seated in the living room, Mr. George took a notebook and pen from his pocket. "Did you see anything unusual yesterday? Anything you thought was out of the ordinary?"

Debra held her hands wide. "I was doing hearing assessments all morning. I didn't see anything."

Lillian folded her hands in her lap. "I was inside the school most of the morning. I stepped outside briefly at morning recess to watch the children and again when I smelled smoke. The children didn't mention seeing anything unusual. I certainly didn't."

But she had. She'd seen a car speeding past. Davey Mast's car. Should she mention that? She didn't want to get anyone in trouble.

"What about the car you saw?" Timothy asked, taking away her option to stay silent.

"When I smelled smoke and went outside, I could see smoke rising from the Hanson farmstead. I heard the explosion and saw flames shooting into the sky. It couldn't have been more than a minute later that I saw Davey Mast drive past."

Sheriff Bradley leaned forward with his elbows propped on his knees. "Are you positive the driver was Davey Mast?"

"I can't say for certain that Davey was driving, but I'm pretty sure it was his car. We saw it the day before. Abe Mast is one of my scholars, one of my students. He said the car belonged to his brother Davey. Has anyone talked to Davey? Perhaps he saw something."

"I have plans to interview him later today." Mr. George tapped his pen against the side of his notebook. "You said we. Who else was with you when you saw Davey's car?"

"All of my students and Timothy the first time I saw it."

"I was giving a fire safety talk at the school," Timothy explained.

Mr. George's sharp gaze came back to Lillian. "And the day of the fire?"

"Susan Yoder was with me. She may have seen the car."

Mr. George nodded, took a few notes and then looked up. "Do you know anyone with a grudge against Mr. Hanson?"

Lillian shook her head. "He isn't a friendly fellow. He and his wife keep to themselves. It's said they don't care much for the Amish."

Mr. George leaned back in his chair. "Why is that?"

Lillian looked at Timothy. "I don't know. Do you?"

"My father said it was something about a land dispute years ago. That's all I know."

"His wife mentioned that he had an argument with an Amish fellow a few days ago. Any idea who that might have been?" the sheriff asked.

Surely he didn't mean her brother. Lillian tried to remember exactly what Jeremiah had said about his conversation with Mr. Hanson. She was certain he hadn't mentioned having an argument, but he did say the man yelled at him. Even if her brother had been arguing with Mr. Hanson, Jeremiah would never retaliate in such a manner. It was unthinkable.

She raised her chin as she met Mr. George's steady gaze. "We Amish go to great lengths to avoid confrontations of any kind. We forgive whoever did this and pray for his soul."

"It's my job to ask questions. I meant no disrespect. Is your brother about?"

"I'm not sure where he is right now. Our parents are

away, and Jeremiah is taking care of my father's business."

"Have you noticed any strangers in the area? Anyone acting suspiciously?" the sheriff asked.

Lillian looked toward her guest. "Miss Merrick is the only stranger I've seen recently."

"There are very few people stranger than I am," Debra said glibly.

Mr. George's face remained stern. "Did you set fire to Mr. Hanson's tractor shed?"

Debra's grin faded. "No. I don't even know the man. My cooking has set off the smoke alarm in my apartment a few times, but that's as close as I've come to being a firebug."

Captain Swanson's cell phone rang. As he answered it, Sheriff Bradley's rang, too. Both men had short, terse conversations and hung up. The captain rose to his feet. "Mr. George, we need to get back to the station house. We have another fire."

Chapter Nine

Timothy shot to his feet when he realized he might be needed with his crew. "Luke has the pager today, but I can come with you."

His captain shook his head. "That won't be necessary. It's a hayfield. No structures involved. One crew should be able to handle it. Thankfully, we don't have the wind today that we had yesterday. I'll drop you off at your place on my way back to the station."

"There's no need. I can walk from here. Whose hayfield is it?"

"Bishop Beachy's." The captain was already moving toward the door.

"Was it deliberately set?" Lillian asked, but he was out the door and didn't answer her.

The fire marshal pulled a business card from his shirt pocket and gave it to Lillian. "Thank you for your time, Miss Keim. If you think of anything else, please get in touch with Captain Swanson. He will know how to contact me. I will get to the bottom of this, I promise. It doesn't matter to me if the arsonist is Amish or not."

Lillian followed them out the door. Timothy joined

her on the porch. As the men drove away, she turned to him with a deeply worried expression on her face. "Your captain doesn't think the fire was started by one of us, does he?"

"By an Amish? *Nee*, I don't think so, but I understand why he has to be sure. Mrs. Hanson is telling people an Amish fellow started it."

"She must be mistaken. I don't know anyone who would endanger the *kinder* so callously."

"I agree. From what I learned on the way over here, the fire was started inside the shed where Mr. Hanson kept his farm equipment. It could be someone wanted to destroy his new tractor. They didn't know or didn't care that he kept extra fuel in there, as well. The resulting explosion along with the high winds allowed the fire to get out of hand quickly."

"I pray whoever started the blaze will see how foolish he was, and I pray he turns to God for forgiveness."

"As do I." He wanted to put his arm around her and pull her close. He wanted to erase the worry he saw in her eyes.

She smiled at him. "Would you like some coffee? There is still some on the stove."

"Not this morning. I have to get back to work. I came along so that you wouldn't feel uncomfortable talking to outsiders."

"I appreciate that you were here."

"That's what friends do," he said softly.

Lillian managed a small smile at Timothy words. "*Ja*, that is what friends do."

Why was it that she suddenly wished they were more than friends? Would he ever see her in any other light?

A red low-slung sports car turned off the highway and drove slowly into the yard. It stopped next to the gate, and a young man rolled down his window. "I'm not sure I'm at the right house. Is Debra Merrick here?"

Lillian was glad of the interruption. "She is, and you must be her brother. I'm Lillian and this is my neighbor Timothy Bowman. Do come in. Debra is inside."

"I'm glad I have the right place. Thanks for taking care of my sister, Miss Keim. I will certainly pay you for your trouble." He opened the car door. It was then Lillian saw how short he was. He needed a thick pad to raise him high enough in the seat to see over the steering wheel.

Timothy moved closer to inspect the vehicle. "Nice car. Electric?"

"Hybrid."

"I see you've made some modifications."

Brandon slipped out of his seat and climbed down. "The foot pedals are the only thing that didn't come standard. They are detachable if my sister or someone of regular height needs to drive."

"No kidding? How do they hook on?" Timothy squatted next to the open door to peer in.

Brandon was soon showing him how to disassemble the pedals. Lillian knew Timothy's curious nature would have him checking under the hood before long. He always wanted to know how things worked. "I'm going to tell Debra you're here."

"We will be right in," Brandon said.

"I won't hold my breath," she answered with a chuckle and walked away.

"What did she mean by that?" Brandon asked.

Timothy grinned. "It means that she knows me pretty

well. Well enough to know I could spend the rest of the morning looking over your vehicle to see how it works."

"Perhaps we should save this for another day. I would hate for my sister to think I'm ignoring her in her hour of need."

"That would be wise."

The small man walked with a rapid rolling gait toward the house, and Timothy followed him. Before they reached the porch, Timothy heard the clip-clop of horses' hooves. A buggy turned off the highway into the lane and came to a stop in front of the house. Timothy's mother stepped down from the driver's seat. Mary and Hannah got out on the other side. Emma and Rebecca got out of the backseat. All of them carried large baskets.

Timothy made the introductions and took his mother's burden from her. He caught a whiff of cinnamon and baked apples. "What have we here?

"Just a little something for Debra so she doesn't have to cook until her ankle is better."

"She should stay off her foot for at least a week," Rebecca added.

Hannah peeked around her mother's skirt at Brandon. "Are you a little person like Amanda?"

"I am," he said with a smile.

"Aren't you going to get any taller?"

"Nope, God made me exactly tall enough. Do you know how I can tell?"

Hannah shook her head. He grinned and pointed down. "Because my feet reach all the way to the ground."

Hannah looked up at her mother. "He's silly."

"Not as silly as you. I see Amanda at the window. Take her some of the cookies you helped me bake."

Timothy held the screen door open for Hannah and

for the women to go inside ahead of him. Rebecca, the last one in line, stopped and whispered in his ear, "I will see which way the wind blows for you. Samuel warned me to be discreet."

Timothy stifled a moan. "Don't say anything. Please. I'm begging you."

She patted his arm. "Your secret is safe with me."

When a hole didn't open up in the floor to swallow him, he reluctantly followed Rebecca inside.

Brandon quickly crossed the room to hug Debra. "You and your adventures. What will you be up to next, sis?"

She returned his embrace. "There's no telling, but as long as I have you to race to my rescue, I'm just going to keep on having them. Thank you for coming so quickly." She sat up a little straighter, wincing as she moved her foot. He took a seat in the wingback chair opposite her.

"I'm just sorry I couldn't get here yesterday. I drove past the school and took some pictures of your car so you can file an insurance claim. I'm sure an adjuster will need to come out and verify the VIN before they pay up. In the meantime, I've arranged to get you a loaner car so you aren't stranded at the apartment."

"Thanks. You're a good brother."

"That's because you're my favorite sister."

"Ha! I'm your only sister."

"Thankfully. Growing up with you around stunted my growth. I'd never have survived another sister."

"You would have ended up two foot four instead of four foot two." They shared a grin that told Timothy it was a long-standing family joke.

Perched on a chair in the corner where he could see into the kitchen, Timothy watched his mother, Mary, Emma and Rebecca as they took over Lillian's kitchen with practiced ease. Lillian and Rebecca were working side by side. He couldn't tell if Rebecca was posing the question to Lillian or not. He hoped she wouldn't find the opportunity, but knowing Rebecca, that was a slim hope at best.

The women soon had coffee cake dished up on plates and glasses filled with iced tea. Lillian carried them into the room and began to pass them out as she introduced everyone. Hannah and Amanda sat quietly at the table, but Timothy could see the girl's interest in Debra's brother.

Brandon accepted a plate and looked at Timothy. "I hope the owner of the cornfield across from the school has crop insurance."

"I'm not sure if he does or not. The Amish do not carry insurance, but Mr. Hanson isn't Amish."

"It's a shame if he didn't have it. I wonder if he would be interested in leasing that acreage to my university. I'm developing a new corn variety and I'm looking for test plots. His field location is excellent. With it burned off, I won't have to deal with any harmful insects, weeds or disease that could be left over in the crop residue. It would make planting there more cost-effective for me. I'd even be willing to put in a cover crop to improve the soil until next spring."

"What kind of cover crop?" Timothy asked.

"I'm a fan of daikon radishes. Their thick roots really improve soil compaction."

Timothy glanced at Lillian and they both started laughing. She held her nose. "I do not want that awful smell surrounding my school for the entire winter."

Brandon blushed bright red. "I'm sorry. I didn't consider that. The smell can be overpowering."

Timothy chuckled. "Our fire station was called out

twice this past winter for a suspected natural gas pipeline leak. It turned out to be the oil radishes in a field across the river from here."

Lillian's chin came up as she leveled a stern look at him. "I had never smelled them before. I had no way of knowing it wasn't a gas leak. I was being civic-minded. There is a pipeline over there."

It was fun to stir that spark of indignation in her eyes. Timothy couldn't help grinning. "True. It was better to be safe than sorry. Why not plant Austrian winter peas as a cover, Brandon?"

"A good choice. I see you have kept up on the advances in no-till farming and soil conservation."

"We read the farm journals," Timothy admitted, trying not to sound offended. Why did people automatically assume that because they used horses they were backward farmers? When a man could only farm so much ground, he had to get the most out of each acre.

"If Mr. Hanson would be willing to lease his ground, I'd write up a lease agreement and get him a check by the end of next week."

Rebecca took a seat beside Debra. "Mr. Hanson is still in the hospital. I'm not sure how you would get hold of Mrs. Hanson. I heard she was staying with one of her sons."

"I'll ask Nick to find out where she is staying," Mary said as she handed Timothy a plate. "Nick Bradley is the sheriff. He and his wife are my adoptive parents," she explained for Debra and Brandon's benefit.

Brandon pulled a business card from his pocket and handed it to her. "My cell phone number is on this. Tell Sheriff Bradley he can call me anytime. Day or night."

"What type of corn are you developing?" Timothy asked.

Debra laughed and held up her hand. "Don't get him started. He will talk about kernel size, drought tolerance and disease resistance all day. This is wonderful coffee cake. I must have the recipe. Which one of you made it?"

"That would be me," his mother said, blushing. "I have put the recipe in the thank-you basket I fixed for you. We know you won't be able to be up and around cooking for a few days, so we put together a few things for you. Consider them a small token of our thanks for helping take care of our *kinder*."

Debra pressed a hand to her chest. "I don't know what to say. Thank you. Lillian did so much more than I did. You should give them to her. I can't accept them."

"But my ankle is fine," Lillian said.

Brandon shook his fork at Debra. "I've seen the inside of your kitchen. I don't want you living on frozen pizza for a week or better. Be thankful and be silent."

In spite of Debra's warning, Timothy wanted to hear more about Brandon's work. "What traits are you trying to produce in your new variety? Is it hard to get the results you want?"

"I warned you." Debra gave her empty plate to Lillian. "Go ahead, Brandon. It's not often you find someone who actually wants to hear about your work."

"You're not in a hurry to get home, are you?" he asked hopefully.

"No, I have enjoyed wearing these same smoky-smelling clothes for two days."

"Okay. Come out to my car, Timothy. I have some of my research data on my laptop. Producing hybrid seed corn isn't difficult, but it is labor-intensive. It requires an understanding of basic genetics, a lot of planning and attention to details, but you don't have to be a genetic engineer to grow your own hybrid seed. To do it yourself, you only need to copy what the seed companies do anyway. Select parent plants with the qualities you want, properly isolate the field to avoid pollen contamination from other sources, manage the seed fields and finally, you have to carefully harvest and store the seed produced."

Timothy couldn't decide if Brandon didn't hear the sarcasm in his sister's voice or if he simply decided to ignore it. "Perhaps another time. I know my father would be interested in your research. We raise a lot of corn for animal feed, but we also sell small amounts of seed corn to other farmers in the area. However, your sister has been through an ordeal and needs your attention today."

"Yes, I would like to go home, brother," Debra said, giving Brandon a no-more-nonsense-from-you look.

Brandon shot his sister a wry smile. "Sorry, you know how I get."

"I do, but I love you anyway."

He rose to his feet. "Timothy, I would like to take a look at your farming operation. Is it all by horse-drawn equipment?"

"For the most part, but we do use some gas-powered machinery we have adapted to be pulled by our horses. You are welcome to stop by anytime. I know your sister was interested in seeing our furniture shop and she wanted to take a look around my mother's gift shop, too, when her foot has healed."

Brandon looked impressed. "Seed corn, furniture, gift shop. It sounds as if your family has diversified past the simple farming I've always associated with the Amish."

"I have four brothers. Two are married and have started families of their own. One more will marry in November. There is only so much land to farm. Not nearly enough to support all of us. My parents were wise enough to seek other ways to provide for their family now and in the future."

"If you think they are only farmers and quilters, you don't know the Amish," Debra said with a wink for Timothy. She sobered and glanced at Lillian. "That was too forward, wasn't it? I told you I wasn't good at meek and humble."

"You are trying, and that is the first step to overcoming any problem," Lillian said gently, holding back a smile.

Debra held out her hand to her brother. "I think I have imposed on this family long enough. Lillian, I'll be back to finish the hearing tests at your school as soon as I am able."

Debra struggled to her feet with his help. Mary and Rebecca were beside her in an instant to help her out to her brother's car. Timothy hung back with his mother, Emma and Lillian.

Brandon looked into the kitchen, where Amanda and Hannah were still sitting. He spoke quietly to Lillian. "My wife and I have adopted two children, both little people, and my daughter looks to be about your sister's age. I would love to meet her."

Had her father been at home, Timothy doubted that he would have permitted it, but Lillian surprised him when she said, "Of course."

She gestured to Amanda. "*Koom* here, *shveshtah*."

Amanda slipped down from her chair and came slowly

into the room. She hid her face in Lillian's skirt. Lillian patted her on the head and looked at Brandon. "My sister doesn't speak English yet. I will translate for you."

"Tell your sister I'm delighted to meet another little person. She is a very pretty little girl."

Lillian relayed the message. Amanda gave him a shy smile, but whispered something to Lillian, making her chuckle. "*Ja,* you are."

"What did she say?" Brandon asked.

"She said she is plain, isn't she? I assured her that she is."

He looked troubled. "I don't understand."

Emma said, "We do not place value on beauty, only on faithfulness to God, commitment to each other and hard work. To tell a girl she is pretty can lead to *gross feelich*, a big feeling. Another way of saying pride."

"I see. Then please ask her if she is an obedient child and minds her sister."

Lillian smiled and translated his question.

Amanda nodded vigorously.

He grinned. "Good. And now I must go and mind my sister or she'll read me the riot act all the way home. Thank you again for taking care of her, Lillian. It was nice meeting all of you. Timothy, I look forward to visiting your farm."

As his mother and Emma went outside with Brandon, Lillian leaned close and whispered in Timothy's ear, "I need to talk to you."

His heart missed a beat. Had Rebecca spoken even after he begged her not to? "Okay. What's up?"

"Later, when we can be alone. Meet me down by the

school after supper." She waved goodbye to Brandon and Debra and then went back inside.

He couldn't tell from her tone or her expression if this meeting was going to be a good thing or not.

Chapter Ten

Lillian sat on one of the chairs she had placed on the school porch and waited nervously for Timothy to arrive. Amanda was happily playing on the swings with two of her dolls. Lillian had hoped Jeremiah would watch their sister this evening, but he hadn't come home. She was starting to worry about him.

Silas had made good on his promise to see about repairs to the school. He and several other men had been finishing the inspection when she and Amanda arrived. It was his feeling that the essential repairs could all be done on Monday, and she agreed.

The sun was hanging low in the sky, turning the bellies of the few clouds gold and red. A light breeze had replaced yesterday's wild wind. It stirred the ashes in the field and carried the smoky smell to her. She marveled once again how merciful God had been toward her and all the children in her charge.

Timothy came walking along the road with long, easy strides. He had his straw hat pulled low on his brow and his hands in his pockets.

"You look deep in thought," she called out.

He paused and looked up, seemingly surprised to see her. He gave her a sheepish grin. "I was."

"Care to share?"

"Not really. What did you need to see me about?" He approached the school and took a seat beside her.

She checked to make sure Amanda couldn't overhear them, and then clasped her hands around her knees. "I'm not sure how to say this, but my brother may have been the Amish man who had an argument with Mr. Hanson. I didn't want to say anything in front of the fire marshal or sheriff, but I had to tell someone."

Her family had always been law-abiding, but distrust of *Englisch* public officials was deeply ingrained and had often been reinforced by her father. Everyone knew that Timothy's brother Joshua had been wrongly imprisoned by the *Englisch* law. It could happen to anyone. The Amish were pacifists and did not resist persecution by outsiders.

Timothy leaned close. "I understand your feelings and I'm glad you know you can talk to me."

"Jeremiah would never try to destroy someone's property. Never. I know he wouldn't. You believe that, don't you?"

"Of course I do. Have you asked him about it?"

She rubbed her palms against each other and wound her fingers tightly together. "He hasn't been home since yesterday. He was upset about Debra staying with us. He said I shouldn't have offered, that Father wouldn't have allowed it. I don't know how to ask him about the argument without sounding as if I'm accusing him of something. Have you learned anything else about the fire?"

He shook his head. "Not about the Hanson fire, but

the fire in Bishop Beachy's hayfield was also deliberately set. The field was a total loss."

"Oh, my! How awful for the bishop, and how awful to think there is an arsonist among us." She wrapped her arms around herself. She wanted to lean against Timothy and draw comfort from his presence, but she knew that wouldn't be modest behavior. "Do the *Englisch* officials have any suspects?"

"Not that they are saying, but I know they recovered some evidence. Luke found a small propane torch that had been left beside a haystack. Luke said it was the same kind Emma sells in her hardware store."

"That doesn't mean it was left by an Amish fellow. Anyone can buy a canister of propane. The *Englisch* use propane, too."

"Burning the bishop's crop makes it seem like someone has a grudge against him. He has very little contact with outsiders. On the other hand, there have been several people shunned by him in the past year."

"Shunned by all of us, not just the bishop. I don't want to believe anyone I know would do such a thing deliberately. It may sound awful, but I hope it turns out to be some *Englisch* vagrant, or wild teenagers, someone I don't know."

"I know what you mean. I feel the same way."

"I'm sure a collection is being taken up to cover the cost of Bishop Beachy's loss."

"*Daed* and *Onkel* Vincent are seeing to it."

The way church members rallied around one of their own in times of trouble was one more wonderful thing about being Amish.

"Was that all you wanted to talk to me about?" Timothy asked, giving her an odd look and then quickly looking away.

If he were one of her students, she would suspect he had done something that he shouldn't. "Were you expecting me to ask about something else?"

"*Nee*, I wasn't. What did you think of Debra's brother today?"

His question seemed forced, as if he were trying deliberately to change the subject. "Brandon seems like a nice fellow. He certainly likes to talk about corn."

Timothy chuckled. "That he does, but he caught my interest. I would like to learn more about producing a hybrid seed. The seed companies charge a premium for hybrid corn. It might be worthwhile to study the technique that Brandon uses so we could produce our own improved varieties."

"He presents it as a practical science, and I'm sure many farmers would be interested in hearing what he has to say." She leaned back against the riser behind her.

"And learning what he has to teach."

"Wouldn't it be wonderful if people like Brandon could present classes to our children?"

He drew back. "You mean invite outsiders into your classroom?"

"*Nee*, but you know what I'm trying to say. Have those people with special knowledge to pass on come in and teach. I sometimes struggle with teaching the older children science and arithmetic. Sometimes I am afraid I'm cheating my students by not giving them a proper education."

"You are a fine teacher. You should not doubt yourself. You have a God-given talent."

"For teaching reading and writing to the little children, but I know I lack the ability to hold the attention of the older ones."

"Just because Abe Mast is a class cutup doesn't mean you are a poor teacher."

"Just inadequate to that challenge."

Timothy slipped his arm around her shoulders and gave her a shake. "Enough with feeling sorry for yourself. I know you, and if there is a way to do something better, you will find it. You haven't been teaching that long. Experience counts."

She managed a smile. "You're right. I will find a better way even if it takes me years. Thanks for your confidence in my ability."

"That's what friends are for."

She gave in and leaned her head against him. "Thank you for being my friend."

She wouldn't allow her feelings for him to get out of hand. Friendship was enough even if there were times when she wished she could offer him more. It wouldn't be fair to him. She wasn't meant to be a wife and a mother.

Timothy breathed in the scent of Lillian. She smelled clean, like spring, like the flowers in his mother's garden early in the morning. It could be the shampoo she used or the soap she washed her clothes with, but whatever it was, he liked it. He wanted to go on holding her, but she soon moved away and he had to let her go. He clasped his hands together to keep from reaching for her again. After having assured her he was a friend, he couldn't start acting like a courting fellow.

He needed to turn his mind to other things. Looking down the south side of the building at the charred and smoke-stained wooden siding that had taken the brunt of the fire's heat, he gestured toward it. "The school needs a coat or two of paint yet."

"It does. We will also need a horse barn and corral before the weather turns cold. The children and I will clean up the school Monday morning and paint this porch if the weather is nice."

"I'll supply the paint and brushes and a ladder or two."

"As always, your help is appreciated." She smiled at him, and his heart missed a beat. If he moved a fraction closer, he could kiss her. Would she let him?

The sound of a car slowing down made them glance toward the road. Davey Mast's red car rolled to a stop beside the school. He stepped out and gave a low whistle. "You sure dodged a bullet, Teacher Lillian."

Dressed in blue jeans and a plaid shirt and wearing a tan cowboy hat over his blond hair, Davey could have passed for an *Englisch* man until he spoke. His Pennsylvania *Deitsch* accent was still strong. Lillian rose to her feet. "It was a near thing. God was good to spare us."

"Jeremiah told me you had a lot to do with saving the school by having the kids wet down the building. Quick thinking."

"You have spoken to Jeremiah today?" she asked.

"In passing. I saw him at the hardware store about an hour ago. No need to threaten him with shunning for spending time with a man under the *bann*."

"You would be welcomed back into our church if you gave up your car and repented breaking your vows to live Amish," Timothy said, still sitting on the steps. "Your own quick thinking spared many homes and farms and we are grateful."

"Not everyone was grateful."

From his sour tone, Timothy guessed Davey was referring to his father. "Many people saw what you did and knew it took courage."

"I had a hot time to be sure. That scorching wind almost turned me into toast. I didn't factor the fire's speed into my equation when I got on that tractor. I might have thought twice about doing it and let the rest of the valley go up in smoke."

"I am glad you didn't. It shows you have a good heart," Lillian said quietly.

He touched the brim of his hat. "That's me. Goodhearted Davey. I'll let you two lovebirds get back to making out on the school steps. Better be careful, Teacher. I happen to know the school board president would take a dim view of such behavior."

"Oh, we weren't…we aren't…" Lillian sputtered to a stop as Davey gave a loud hoot of laughter.

Timothy caught her hand. "Don't mind him. He likes to stir up trouble. He always has."

"Tell your brother Luke I sure miss partying with him. He knew how to have a good time. It's a shame he's been brainwashed back into the fold. You might mention there's a barn party over at Abram Coblentz's farm tonight and he's welcome. I'll have the good stuff there." With that parting shot, Davey got back in his car and roared away.

Lillian crossed her arms over her chest. "Just when I was starting to feel sorry for him. Do you think he will tell his father about us?"

Timothy laid a hand on her shoulder. "*Nee*, it was an empty threat, and I doubt Silas would believe such a thing of you. But it is getting late and we should both be getting home."

"You're right. What is your family doing tomorrow?"

It was an off Sunday, the Sunday without the biweekly church meeting. Most families used the day to go visiting or have family over, and his was no exception. "We are going to visit my mother's brother over by Longford. Everyone except Samuel and Rebecca. She has asked John Miller and his mother over. They were her in-laws before she married Samuel, and they remain close."

"I remember her first husband. He was a *goot* man. It was a shame he died so young, but God had a plan for the wife he left behind."

"He did, and my brother Samuel is grateful he was part of that plan. What about you?"

"We have been invited to visit our aunt and uncle in Hope Springs. Father had arranged for a driver to take us before he and *Mamm* had to leave to be with father's uncle. I almost decided to cancel the trip after the fire, but I think Amanda needs to be with her cousins. Two of them are little people, and she has so much fun when they get together."

"It will be good for you to get away, too. Have you heard from your parents?"

"Not yet. I expect a letter by Monday letting me know how things stand. I pray they were able to make it before my great-uncle passed. When we first moved to Wisconsin, it was so my father could work with my uncle in his construction business. They had a falling-out several years later, and that was the reason we moved back here. I pray they were able to make amends. I know my father deeply regretted the split."

"Will you be traveling there for the funeral?"

"*Nee*, it is too far, and I would not want to miss that much school. I would fall even further behind in my homework. I have not had a chance to open the book you gave me. Would you like it back?"

"Keep it as a token of my friendship and read it when you have the chance. I know you'll enjoy it. What time should I show up with the paint?"

"First thing Monday morning."

"Until then." He tipped his hat and started walking away. She watched him until he reached the bend in the road. He turned round and lifted a hand in a brief wave. She resisted the urge to call him back, to spend a little more time in his company. Instead, she waved, too. When he was out of sight, she went to get Amanda and together they started for home.

When she reached the house, she saw Jeremiah sitting on the bench on the front porch. His horse and buggy waited at the gate. He rose to his feet. "Where have you been?"

"I went to the school to check on the repairs that were done today. Where have you been?"

"Visiting a friend."

His brusque reply annoyed her. "Amanda, go in and start getting ready for bed." When her sister went into the house, Lillian rounded on Jeremiah. "Does this friend have a name?"

He strode past her. "I'm going out. Don't wait up for me."

"The driver taking us to Hope Springs will be here tomorrow at eight o'clock."

"I won't be going with you." He climbed into his buggy.

She followed him and put a hand on the buggy door. "Jeremiah, what is going on?"

"I'm sick of work, work, work. I'm going to go have a little fun."

"With Davey Mast? I saw him tonight and he told me there is going to be a barn party at Abram Coblentz's farm."

"You're welcome to come along. You might enjoy letting your hair down for once in your life."

"I had my *rumspringa*, and I took my vows. I hold to them. You have been baptized, too. You should put your running around years behind you before you find yourself in serious trouble."

"In serious trouble with who? Our stuffy old bishop? He won't be spying on anyone tonight," he said with a chuckle.

"What's that supposed to mean?"

"Didn't you hear? There was a fire in his hayfield."

"I did hear. The sheriff and the fire marshal were here today asking questions about the fire at the Hanson Farm when they got the call."

Her brother's grin disappeared, replaced by deep scowl. "What kind of questions?"

"Mrs. Hanson told the sheriff an Amish man had an argument with her husband the day before the fire. They asked if I knew who that Amish man might be."

"What did you tell them?"

"Nothing. Even if you were the one Mr. Hanson had an argument with, I know you had nothing to do with the fire."

"I appreciate your blind loyalty, sister."

"It isn't blind. I know you as well as I know myself."

"I have to get going. I don't want to miss my ride."

"I wish you wouldn't go."

"I have to. It's a goodbye party for Davey Mast. He's moving away."

"Where is he going?"

"Philadelphia. Who knows when I'll see him again? Give Aunt Sarah and Uncle Howard my love and tell Cousin Ben he still owes me ten dollars." He snapped the reins to set the horse in motion and Lillian was forced to move aside.

She was more troubled than she cared to admit. She spent a long time on her knees praying for her brother that night and for Davey Mast. When she finally slipped beneath the pink-and-white-stitched quilt, her thoughts turned to Timothy. Alone in her room she faced her growing feelings for him and wrestled with what to do about them.

Her common sense said she needed to spend less time in his company and put some emotional distance between them. Her heart said otherwise. The memory of being held in his arms sent a pulse of warmth across her skin.

She pressed her hands over her eyes. This was completely ridiculous. They were friends and they would stay friends. She would recover from this emotional upheaval caused by her fright during the fire in a week or two. Until then, she would make sure she wasn't alone with him again. She would keep her guard up when he was near.

Turning over on her side, she pulled the quilt to her chin, determined to fall asleep. She did, only to dream of Timothy's bright smile and easy laughter. She woke with a vague feeling of happiness but quickly came to her senses.

Throwing the quilt back, she got out of bed determined not to see Timothy or dream about him again.

Chapter Eleven

Early Monday morning, a gallon of white paint in one hand and a stepladder balanced on his shoulder, Timothy headed across the covered bridge toward the school. Behind him came Joshua and Mary with Emma and Luke. Hannah skipped along ahead of them. The adults all carried supplies to help clean and paint the schoolhouse. While Timothy had enjoyed visiting with his relatives the day before, he was eager to see Lillian again. It was a little frightening how much he had missed her.

"What's the rush, *bruder*?" Luke called out.

Timothy realized he was several long strides ahead of the group. He stopped and waited for them to catch up. "I'm not in a rush. You just like to dawdle, Luke. The sooner we get started, the sooner we will be finished."

"And the sooner you can spend more time with that certain someone." Luke winked as he walked past.

Timothy turned his face to the sky, closed his eyes and shook his head. He never should have mentioned anything about Lillian to his irreverent brother.

"Don't tease him, Luke," Emma warned, giving her fiancé a stern look.

Timothy sent her a grateful look. At least he had someone on his side. "*Danki*, Emma."

"You won't let me have any fun," Luke said with an exaggerated pout.

She took his hand. "If you don't behave yourself, you will be walking home alone. Is that what you want?"

"I'll behave. I promise." Luke pressed her hand to his lips.

"Not much chance of that," Joshua called out. "*Mamm* will tell you Luke hasn't behaved since he was two years old."

"That's not so. I was a good kid. I got blamed for a lot of things you and Timothy did."

"Like what?" Timothy asked.

Luke stopped in front of Joshua. "Like the time the milk cows broke through the fence and scattered all over creation because someone threw firecrackers under their feet. Remember that, little *bruder*?"

Joshua stabbed his finger into Luke's chest. "Who gave me the firecrackers, lit them for me and told me where to toss them? You were older, and you should have known better."

Timothy laughed. "I believe those were *Daed*'s exact words when he settled on your punishment, Luke."

He grimaced. "And I still hate okra to this day. I had to harvest the biggest patch *Mamm* ever planted. Okra has little spines all over the leaves and stems. They stuck in my skin and itched for days."

"You are supposed to wear gloves and heavy long sleeves," Mary said.

"*Mamm* told me that, but I was in a hurry to get done and get to a softball game. Big mistake."

Hannah had stopped up the road waiting for them. "Hurry up. I don't want to be late to school."

"Go ahead without us, *liebchen*," her father said.

She took off at a run. Timothy knew exactly how she felt. He wanted to run ahead, too.

The school was already a beehive of activity by the time they arrived. Three men on ladders were scraping away the damaged paint on the south side. Lillian was standing on a smaller stepladder between two of them washing a window. Just seeing her made Timothy's morning brighter.

Emma and Mary went inside with their cleaning supplies. Luke and Joshua headed to check out the burned-out car that still sat beside what was left of the horse barn.

Timothy approached Lillian and stopped beside her. "*Guder mariye.* Timothy Bowman reporting for his assignment, Teacher Lillian."

"Good morning." She wiped her brow on her sleeve. She didn't smile the way she always smiled at him. She didn't even look at him.

She returned to scrubbing the glass without even a glance in his direction. "Silas is in charge of the men. Check with him. I believe he's by the old barn."

"Are you okay?" he asked. Something didn't feel right.

"I'm fine. Just busy." She kept scrubbing at a spot near the top of the window.

"Okay, I'll get to work." He walked away but glanced back once. She didn't look his way. What had happened to upset her between the time they parted on Saturday and this morning?

"Timothy, why don't you and your brothers start painting the porch?" Silas said, gesturing in the direction.

Timothy nodded and joined Luke and Joshua. As they

set up two ladders, he opened the paint can and handed out the brushes. His brothers took them and dipped them in the pail. Timothy stared at the step where he'd put his arm around Lillian. It had been more than a friendly gesture on his part. Did she realize that? Was that what upset her? Or was something wrong at home? She'd been worried about her brother lately.

Timothy glanced toward Silas. Perhaps Davey had made good on his threat and reported what he thought he saw to his father. Had Silas berated her for unseemly behavior?

"What's the matter?" Luke asked.

Timothy wished his brother wasn't quite so observant. "I'm not sure, but I think Lillian is giving me the cold shoulder."

"What did you do?"

Timothy shook his head. "I don't know. She wasn't upset with me when I saw her last."

"Then maybe it isn't you and she simply has other things on her mind."

"You're probably right." He was making a big deal out of nothing. She wants to get the school opened for the children again as soon as possible. And now he was the one dawdling. He dipped his brush in the paint and set to work.

By noon, the school had been cleaned inside and out. The windows shone brightly. The siding and the new porch gleamed with the still wet paint. A half dozen more buggies arrived along with several pony carts filled with older women, including his mother. Colorful quilts were spread under the trees that had been spared by the blaze at the back of the property, and families were soon gathered around picnic hampers. Happy chatter and shrieks of childish laughter filled the air, as children who had been painting, scrubbing the floor and raking debris were free to play on the swings and teeter-totter. A few boys and young men had gotten up a softball game.

Timothy was about to join them when he noticed a wagon coming in loaded with lumber. Jeremiah Keim was at the reins. He stopped by the burned-out barn. Silas Mast spoke briefly with him, and then motioned for Timothy to join them.

"Jeremiah has donated the lumber for the new horse barn. Will you help him unload it?"

"Sure. Jeremiah, have you eaten?" Timothy asked.

"Not yet." Jeremiah's gaze was fixed on his sister. She was busy cleaning white paint off Amanda's hands and hadn't noticed him.

"Come over and join us. My mother always brings way too much food."

"I will unless Lillian has something for me." He started to get down from the wagon.

"Tell her that she and Amanda are welcome to join us, too." Timothy walked away without waiting to see what Lillian's response was. Lillian had made a point of avoiding him all morning. He figured if she was truly upset with him, and he had no idea why she would be, then she wouldn't join them. If they were still friends, she would take the invitation at face value and come enjoy the company of his family.

He passed up the ball game and went to sit on his mother's quilt. He was pleased a few minutes later when Amanda came over to sit beside Hannah. Lillian and Jeremiah soon followed. Lillian began setting out the ham and bread she had brought for sandwiches. She still wouldn't look at him. As he knew his mother would, she produced a mountain of food in plastic bowls and jars. Along with paper plates and utensils, she placed everything in the center of the blanket. The fried chicken, German potato salad, pickles, pickled beets, a stack of brownies and two jugs of fresh lemonade left little room for people to sit.

She made sure everyone had a heaping plate of food on their lap before she sat down with a sigh and leaned back against the tree trunk. She gazed out over the families gathered together. "It does this old heart good to see so many people willing to help."

"Not as many as usual," Mary said. "I've noticed everyone scanning the horizons looking for signs of smoke. I know I have been. I think every family has left at least one member home to keep an eye on their place."

Emma took a piece of ham and put it on her plate. "People are watching strangers closely. I've even been uneasy when someone I don't know stops at our store."

The threat was why there were fewer people helping today. Timothy's father and Noah had remained at home, since Noah was carrying the fire pager and had wanted to stay near the highway in case he was called out.

Emma passed around a tray of deviled eggs. "I'm sure many folks have gone to deliver hay to Bishop Beachy and take donations to his family. His buggy horse was in the pen closest to the blaze. It bolted in panic, tried to jump the fence and broke a leg. The vet couldn't save it and the poor thing had to be put down."

"How awful." Lillian's eyes glistened with tears. She cared almost as much about animals as she did about the children in her care.

"To buy a well-trained horse broke to harness can cost over a thousand dollars. It's no small expense. The bishop doesn't have deep pockets." Luke handed the tray of eggs back to Emma minus the three he'd added to his plate.

Timothy's mother poured herself a glass of lemonade. "Isaac has lent him one of our horses until he is able to purchase another. Our congregation will give what they can to make up for his loss just as they are giving to repair this school. Did you boys know your great-great-grandfather donated this land and helped to build this school?"

Timothy nodded. "I heard the story a long time ago when Grandfather was still alive."

"I don't think I've heard it," Luke said.

"*Ja*, you did," Joshua and Timothy said together.

"Well, I don't remember it."

Timothy flicked Luke's hair. "Because you weren't paying attention. As usual."

Their mother smiled. "Grandfather Bowman wanted his children to have a better education than he had. In his time, there weren't so many Amish in this area. He went to public school, but he was teased and bullied there. It was during the First World War and many *Englisch* resented the fact that the Amish wouldn't serve in the military. So he built a school for his own children, all fourteen of them, and hired an Amish teacher."

"We are grateful for his generous deed," Lillian said. "Many Amish children have benefited because of it."

Joshua gestured toward Jeremiah's wagon. "That load of lumber is a substantial donation from your family, Jeremiah."

"We can afford it." Jeremiah reached for another chicken leg, adding it to his plate.

Timothy caught the sharp glance Lillian shot her brother but she didn't say anything. Timothy knew her father's construction business along with her teaching salary was barely enough to support the family. While Amish families were expected to help one another, they weren't compelled to give more than they could afford. If there were more fires in their Amish community, it would put a strain on everyone.

"Who do you think is behind these fires?" Mary asked the question many of them were thinking.

"Someone with a grudge against the two men, maybe. Mrs. Hanson said her husband had an argument with an Amish fellow. She didn't know his name. The fire marshal hopes when Mr. Hanson is able to speak, he can name the man." Timothy pinned his gaze on Jeremiah, waiting to see his reaction. In his heart, he didn't believe Jeremiah was an arsonist. Timothy's faith required him to see good in every man, but he had heard Lillian's concerns and wanted to ease her fears.

Jeremiah looked at his sister. She bit her lower lip. He put his plate down and met Timothy's gaze. "I had a quarrel with Mr. Hanson the day before the fire, if you can call it that. All the shouting was done by him. I offered to harvest his corn for a fair price. I heard that he'd fired the crew he hired last month."

Luke leaned toward Jeremiah. "Then there were others who might have a grudge against him. Do you know who they were?"

Jeremiah's gaze shifted away. "I will not cast even the shadow of blame on another man."

"I don't see how a harvest crew could have a grudge against Bishop Beachy," Joshua said.

Timothy's mother heaved a deep sigh. "We may never know who has done these things. We must pray for them. We must ask God to open their eyes and hearts and allow them to see the error of their ways. Only God knows what is in the heart of a man. He is the ultimate judge."

They all nodded in agreement. The rest of the meal passed in silence. When everyone was through eating, the women were soon deep in conversation discussing plans for Luke and Emma's upcoming wedding as they gathered up the plates and flatware. Lillian smiled and added a few comments, but Timothy could see she was still distracted. Something was troubling her. Something more than her brother's argument with Mr. Hanson. Timothy wanted to find out what was wrong, but he couldn't do that in front of everyone.

He rose to his feet. "I think I need to walk off some of *Mamm*'s good fried chicken before I get back to work. Anyone care to join me?" He stared directly at Lillian.

For a second, Lillian looked as if she would, but then a shadow came into her eyes. She shook her head and looked away. "I must get back inside. I have paperwork to catch up on."

His spirits plummeted. For whatever reason, she was determined to avoid him. He racked his brain for the cause and came up with only one answer. He had overstepped the bounds of friendship by putting his arm around her.

Seeing Timothy's crestfallen expression tore at Lillian's heart. Her determination to avoid being alone with him was hurting him as much as it was hurting her. That was never her intention.

Joshua stood up. "I'll take a walk with you, Timothy. I'd like to take a better look at the Hanson Farm and see if there is anything our family can do to help."

"The old man doesn't want help from the Amish," Jeremiah said, an edge of bitterness in his tone.

The Bowman men looked shocked. Timothy said, "He may not want our help, but that doesn't mean we should ignore him."

"The *Englisch* have insurance that pays them well for their losses. They don't need our help." Jeremiah stomped away from the group.

Lillian shot to her feet. "Jeremiah didn't mean that. I've changed my mind about that walk, Timothy. I will come with you. I would like to see the damage, too. If there *is* something we can do, the family doesn't need to know the help came from us."

"Why is your brother so bitter toward the *Englisch*?" Mary asked.

Lillian sighed. Her family had never shared the story of their experiences, but perhaps it was time they did. "When our family moved to Wisconsin, Jeremiah and our father went to work for our father's uncle. Uncle Albert ran a construction business. It was a very successful business. Amish and *Englisch* alike appreciated the quality of work they produced. After a few years, Uncle Albert put my father in charge at the building sites and stayed in his office. He was getting on in years. Father was almost finished framing a fancy house for a rich *Englisch* fellow when the man decided the work wasn't up to his standards. He refused to pay for the materials and time my father put in."

"How awful. That wasn't right," Mary said.

"A few days later, the home caught fire in the night and burned to the ground. The man blamed Father. He said the Amish didn't know how to work around electricity and that they had caused a short in the wiring. He refused to pay for the building materials and tools that were lost. He sued Uncle Albert and won. It was a huge blow to the business. Uncle Albert felt Father was partly to blame. It caused a split in the family. We found out later the homeowner had collected a tidy sum of insurance. He didn't need the money he got from the lawsuit to cover his loses. He ended up building a much bigger house."

"Not all *Englisch* are greedy," Ana said. "We have many *Englisch* friends who live upright lives and are faithful to God."

"I know that. I try to live my faith." Lillian had harbored bitterness for a time, but she was able to forgive the man when she realized her bitterness was only hurting her, not him.

"Was the cause of the fire ever determined?" Timothy asked.

Something in his tone made her look closely at him. She had tried to forget that stressful time and put it all behind her. "I'm not sure. Why?"

Timothy smiled at her. "Just wondering, that's all. I am a fireman, even if only a volunteer."

"Timothy is the curious one, Lillian," Luke said. "You should know that about him."

"Jeremiah may know." She caught the glance the Bowman brothers shared and wondered at it.

"I think I'll ask him about it," Luke said, and walked away to where Jeremiah was unloading the wagon.

Ana had Mary help her to her feet. "Let's get the quilts folded up and get home. I have a mountain of mending to do."

"I'll help," Lillian said.

Ana shooed her away with the wave of a hand. "*Nee,*

take your walk. You have done enough this morning. I can manage."

"All right." Lillian glanced over her shoulder to where Luke stood talking to Jeremiah. The glare Jeremiah cast in her direction told her he wasn't happy that she had shared their family's story. He unhitched his horse from the wagon, got on the mare and rode away.

A fire there and now fires here. There couldn't possibly be a connection, could there?

Chapter Twelve

Timothy noticed Lillian's unease as she stared after her brother. She was clenching and unclenching her fingers tightly together. Something was wrong between them. He hoped and prayed her brother wasn't involved in these fires.

Joshua held out his hand to his wife. "Let's take that walk, shall we? I saw a car pull into the Hansons' lane a few minutes ago."

Mary smiled at him. "I need to get something from your mother's buggy first."

Timothy followed them. Lillian made sure Amanda knew where she was going and left her under the watchful eyes of Susan Yoder, and then Lillian joined Timothy, Mary and Joshua.

Mary pulled out another heavy-looking basket from the back of the buggy. Joshua took in from her and settled it in the crook of his arm.

"I need to get something from the school, too," Lillian said, and hurried away.

She rejoined them with a smaller basket over her arm. Timothy took it from her and the couples began walking side by side down the road. Timothy let his brother get a little way in front of them and looked at Lillian. "Are you okay?"

"A little tired."

"You worked like a beaver this morning."

"I feel responsible for getting everything done."

He wanted her to share what was troubling her even if it didn't reflect well on him. "I thought maybe something had happened that upset you."

She gave him a shy smile. "Is that your way of telling me that I've been cranky?"

"Don't go putting words in my mouth." At least she was beginning to sound like her old self.

"I'm sorry. I was out of sorts this morning."

"It's understandable. Many disturbing things have happened. But look on the bright side. You got the school painted two years ahead of time, and you are getting a new barn. I know you had complained to Silas that the old one had a leaky roof. Now I won't have to fix it."

"The school does look nice. Once the charred grass grows back, it will look like nothing has ever happened. I hope it entices one of our young women to step forward and take the new teacher position."

"I thought the school board hadn't decided if they were going to hire another teacher."

"I overheard some of the board members talking, and they are in favor of giving me the extra help."

"That's *goot.*"

"For me and for my scholars." They had reached the lane that ran up to the Hanson farmstead. A man was posting a large No Trespassing sign on the fence.

Joshua stepped forward. "Can you tell us how Mr. and Mrs. Hanson are doing?"

The man folded his arms with the hammer still in his hand. "My grandparents have lost their home. How do you think they are?"

His tone and stance told Timothy he wasn't willing to be friendly. "You're Billy. I remember going fishing with you when we were little. You caught five nice catfish, and I didn't catch a thing."

The man's face softened. "Timmy, right? I remember you."

Lillian took the basket from Timothy and handed it to the man. "I'm Lillian Keim, the teacher at the school up the road. We are all sorry about what happened and the children wanted to help. They have put together a few things for your grandparents. Could you see that they get them?"

He hesitated and then took the basket from her. "Sure."

"We have something for them, too." Mary took her basket from Joshua and held it out. Billy laid his hammer on the post behind grasp the handles. "That's good of you folks. I'll admit it's unexpected. Granddad didn't care much for the Amish. I thought the feeling was mutual."

"We believe in helping our neighbors," Mary said shyly, and stepped back.

"If you really want to help, find out which one of your people did this. Don't just forgive them and let them get away with it." Billy's voice quivered with some strong emotion.

Mary laid a hand on his arm. "My father is Sheriff Bradley. He's a just man. He will uncover the truth. He doesn't play favorites."

"I can attest to that," Joshua said with a smile for his wife. "Nick threw me in jail not long after we met."

"And he let you out when he discovered you were innocent," Mary added.

Billy cleared his throat. "It's good to know the sheriff doesn't believe the Amish are above reproach. Thanks for this stuff. I'll see that Grandma gets it. Granddad is still in the hospital, but he should get out in a few days."

"We are praying for his speedy recovery," Lillian said gently.

"Thanks. Were any of the kids at the school hurt?"

"They were frightened, but the children are fine," Lillian assured him.

"Good." Billy turned away, but turned back after a few steps. "It takes a sick man to destroy someone's home and livelihood for no reason. My grandparents are getting too old to start over."

Lillian took a quick step forward. "Sir, do you think your grandfather would be interested in leasing his cornfield to Ohio Central University? Professor Brandon Merrick is seeking land to lease for a new hybrid corn test plot. He says they pay well and quickly."

"Ohio Central? I'll talk to Granddad about it. He's worried about money. They had insurance on the house, but not on the crops."

"This might be a way to help them," Timothy said.

Billy walked away with his head down and his shoulders bowed.

Timothy sent up a prayer for him and for his family.

Joshua took Mary's hand. "Let's go home, since we are almost there. I don't want to leave *Daed* with all the work that needs to be done in the shop today."

"I'll tell Hannah where you've gone and make sure she gets home," Timothy said.

Mary smiled and nodded. *"Danki."*

The pair left and continued walking toward the river hand in hand.

"Those two make me want to get married," Timothy said softly, looking into Lillian's eyes.

Lillian avoided Timothy's intense gaze. "They seem like a happily married couple. God has blessed them."

"God has blessed three of my brothers with pearls beyond price."

"If it is His will, you will be blessed as well in God's own time. We should get back to the school. I am hoping to hold classes this afternoon. The children need to know things are back to normal."

Timothy gestured toward the blackened field where a few charred pieces of corn stubble stood as a mute reminder of that frightening day. "It isn't exactly normal. They all have to walk past this reminder morning and night."

Lillian started walking. "Are you simply curious about the cause of the fire in Wisconsin, or are you looking for a connection to these fires?"

"I was curious, but you have to admit it is odd that your brother had angry words with both men involved."

"He has never had angry words with Bishop Beachy."

"That we know about."

"You can't suspect him, Timothy. He wouldn't do this."

"I don't believe he did, but I think you have some suspicions, as well."

She stopped and turned to face him. "I do and I am so ashamed of that. He is my brother."

"I know how you feel. When we first learned that

Luke was using and selling drugs, none of us believed it. We were wrong."

"You weren't wrong to believe in him. He repented and became a stalwart member of our faith. Your belief in him was justified."

"I pray that your faith in Jeremiah is justified, as well. I really don't want to think that one of us is behind this. It goes against everything I cherish. Is that the only thing troubling you, or is there something else? I hope you know you can tell me anything. I'm your friend. If my behavior the other evening has upset you, just tell me."

Lillian glanced at him from the corner of her eye. He had his hands in his pockets. His shoulders were slumped and his hat rode low on his forehead. Having seen the same expression on some of her students when they knew they were in trouble, she couldn't help smiling. "We have always been at ease with each other. Perhaps too much so."

"You are upset with me. I thought as much."

"I know you were only trying to comfort me, but not everyone would view it that way. I can't afford to lose my job. The more I thought about Davey's comment, the more convinced I became that our relationship could be viewed in the wrong context."

"It was less complicated being friends when we were young. All I had to worry about then was being teased by my brothers for hanging out with a girl."

"Many things were easier when we were young."

"I value your friendship, Lillian. I would never do anything to hurt you. The next time you need some comfort, I'll send Hannah to give you a hug."

"And I will send back a hug to you in the same fashion."

"*Goot.* Now that we have that out in the open and settled, can you smile at me once in a while?"

She couldn't hold back a grin. "If you insist."

"*Danki,* I feel much better now."

So did Lillian. She wouldn't have to avoid Timothy. He understood that their friendship was open to scrutiny and had to remain circumspect. She was the one who needed to remind herself of that fact. Because being alone with Timothy was like wading in the river. She never knew when she might step into a hole and find the water was over her head without warning.

A long day of soaking rain on Wednesday put an end to the dry spell and decreased the fire danger in the community. When there hadn't been another incident by the time Sunday services rolled around, Lillian and many others began to relax.

She helped Amanda into the family's black buggy, cleaned and washed for the occasion. Jeremiah drove his open-topped courting buggy, a sign he hoped to take one of the local girls home later that day. Lillian didn't think there was anyone special in her brother's life, but she didn't know for sure. Jeremiah had grown tight-lipped in the past few months. Maybe there was a girl.

The service was being held at the home of Isaac and Ana Bowman. Members of the community took turns hosting the bimonthly preaching service but never more than once a year to prevent it becoming a burden on any one family. Hosting the service required a great deal of preparation. Family members and friends gathered several days before to clean the house inside and out. Pies and cakes were baked to be served at the luncheon where nearly one hundred people would gather after the service. Cookies, brownies, punch and other treats were prepared for the young people who would stay until late in the evening to socialize and enjoy a singing.

Inside the Bowman home, the walls between the lower rooms had been opened up to make room for rows of backless benches. The early-morning sunshine poured in through spotless windows and cast low rectangles across the polished wooden floor. Women sat together on one side while the men sat across the aisle. Since the married women normally sat together, Lillian and Amanda sat behind them with the single women and young girls.

A visiting bishop arrived to help with the preaching, since Lillian's father had not yet returned. He turned out to have a great gift for speaking and everyone present felt his words were guided by the Holy Spirit. Following the three-hour service, the visitor gave a plea for help with one of his parishioner's medical bills. Their teenage son had been diagnosed with leukemia and his medical expenses were mounting. Donations were collected for that family, and then the minister passed the collection plate for Bishop Beachy. Lillian gave what she could but knew it was a pitifully small amount. Bishop Beachy then announced the banns of marriage for two young couples from the congregation. Neither of them was a big surprise.

Afterward, Lillian sent Amanda to play with several other young children under the watchful eyes of their mothers and then joined the women helping serve the light luncheon inside. The backless benches had been stacked together to make a half dozen narrow tables. The congregation ate in shifts with deference being given to the elders first. The teenagers and young children would eat last. The arrangement suited them, as it gave them more time to spend with their friends.

Lillian took her place washing dishes at the sink. Rebecca was helping her dry them. Ana came in and handed Lillian a tray of glasses. "I see your parents have not yet returned. Have you had word from them?"

"I had a letter on Friday. *Onkel* has rallied, and Father wishes to remain for the time being. They dearly miss Amanda. Mother regrets not taking her with them, but they never expected to be gone so long."

"Are you and your brother coping without them?" Rebecca asked.

"We are, although I think Jeremiah prefers Mother's cooking over mine."

Rebecca laughed. "Samuel never complains, but I know he prefers Ana's cooking."

"He has never said such a thing to me," Ana declared. "He says you are a *goot* cook."

"He eats two helpings of your meat loaf and he'll only take one of mine."

"I will write out my recipe for you, if you like," Ana offered.

Rebecca set her hands on her hips and stretched backward, making her rounded belly stick out even farther. "I would rather come over and eat yours. It's easier. I've been too tired to do much cooking lately."

Ana patted Rebecca's tummy. "I will make up some meals for you this week. You need your rest. This baby will be here in no time, and then rest will be out of the question."

Ana went back to gather more dishes. Rebecca frowned and pressed a hand to her ribs as she stretched sideways. "I wish he would find a new place to kick me. I must be black and blue on the inside on this rib."

"You look happy in spite of that." Lillian refused to

dwell on the fact that she would never be a mother, but sometimes, like now, a stab of jealously hit her hard. She willed it away.

Rebecca laced her fingers together over her stomach. "I am happy and yet I'm also afraid of that happiness. I know how easily it can be taken away."

"To worry is to doubt God," Lillian said, quoting one of the many Amish proverbs she'd heard all her life.

"You're right. God is good. I will trust the kindness of the Lord, for He has given me many blessings. Do you ever think about getting married, Lillian? I know you love teaching and you do a wonderful job with the *kinder*, but what if someone was interested in courting you? Would you be open to the idea?"

"Are you talking about someone specific or in general terms?" Lillian handed her friend another plate to dry, wondering if Timothy had put Rebecca up to this.

Rebecca rubbed the saucer slowly with her towel. "I'm speaking in general terms."

Which meant Rebecca would become more specific if Lillian admitted to being open to the idea. "In general terms, I love my job and I have no wish to give it up."

"Even for the love of a husband and children of your own?"

Lillian didn't normally have a problem denying her desire for love and marriage, but today the words stuck in her throat. If things were different. If she could give Timothy the family he wanted—but she couldn't. "I love the children I teach, and that is enough for me. Someday the right man may come along. No one can know God's plan. Until then, teaching holds sway over my heart."

She could almost imagine marrying a widower who needed help raising a half dozen children, but even then it would be a poor bargain for the man because her heart belonged to Timothy.

She kept her head down and vigorously scrubbed a sticky pan, hoping no one noticed the tear that slipped down her cheek before she could blink it back.

Chapter Thirteen

Lillian was delighted to see Debra and Brandon when they stopped by just as she was leaving the school on Tuesday afternoon. Debra, balancing on crutches, came around the front of her brother's car wearing a cast on her foot.

Lillian pressed a hand to her chest. "Don't tell me your foot was broken. You poor thing."

Debra extended her cast. "One small bone is all. This monstrosity makes it look worse than it is."

"I'm so sorry."

"It wasn't your fault, Lillian. It was my own clumsiness. How are you? How are all the children? Are any of you having difficulties with PTS?"

Lillian tipped her head. "With what?"

"Post-traumatic stress. Nightmares, excessive worrying, trouble concentrating, things that can happen to people after a frightening experience."

"Several of the *kinder* have told me they were scared to come back to school at first, but they seem okay now. Are you having such troubles?"

Debra shrugged. "A few nightmares, but they're getting better."

"I'm glad."

Debra moved toward the school. "I'm amazed. The building doesn't look like it just came through a fire. If it wasn't for the charred field across the way, I would think I was at the wrong school."

Lillian smiled broadly. "Our community comes together to help when there is trouble. We missed only one day of school. The paint, lumber and labor was all donated by the families of our children. The barn was rebuilt, too, but I'm afraid we couldn't do anything with your car."

"Hasn't my insurance company been here to tow it away?"

"Not yet."

Brandon folded his arms over his chest. "We can't get our insurance company to come pick up one car while in the same amount of time you folks have restored your school and built a barn. Something is wrong with that picture."

Debra hobbled toward the steps. "I'm telling you, Brandon, I'm going to become Amish. These people have the right idea about a lot of things."

Brandon laughed. "The only thing standing in your way is that you like driving, you love electricity, you couldn't live without your computer and you can't cook."

"Details, details. Lillian, I need my notes and to download the results from the machine I left behind. Are they still here?"

"I've kept your equipment and notes in the coatroom. I thought perhaps the health department would send someone to finish the tests, but I haven't heard from them."

"I'll be here Friday morning to complete them. I don't

have to stand to do hearing screens, so my supervisor is letting me come back to work half days. I still can't drive, but Brandon has agreed to haul me out here and back."

"*Wunderbar* and so kind of him."

"Don't go assuming he is the kindly older brother. He has an ulterior motive."

Brandon gestured toward the burned cropland. "I spoke with Mr. Hanson, and he has leased his acreage to me for a test field. Thanks to you, I take it. Mr. Hanson's grandson told me you were the one who mentioned it."

"I was happy to do something that would benefit both of you."

"You'll be seeing a lot of me over the spring and summer months. I wanted to ask if you thought some of your students would be interested in earning extra money working for me next summer."

"Detasseling the corn? I'm sure they will."

Debra threw one hand in the air, almost dropping her crutch. "See how smart this woman is? I had no idea what detasseling was, and she knew right off the bat. What is it, anyway?"

Lillian suppressed a grin. "Detasseling is a form of pollination control. By removing the pollen-producing flowers, what we call the tassel, from the tops, the plant can't fertilize itself as corn normally does. Pollen is carried by the wind from adjacent plants of a different corn variety onto the silks of the forming ears. This produces a cross-breed or hybrid. They tend to be stronger and produce a better yield than either parent."

"An excellent explanation," Brandon said.

"I confess I have only recently read up on the subject," Lillian admitted. "Timothy lent me some of the farm journals he gets."

"I hope to get a cover crop planted in the next few weeks. Austrian winter peas, not daikon radishes."

Lillian tipped her head. "Thank you for that."

"I was also hoping to hire someone local to care for the field. By that, I mean plant the ground cover, cultivate, fertilize, monitor growth stages and that type of thing. Any suggestions?"

The project would be something Timothy would enjoy, but she wanted to offer the job to her brother first. They could use the extra income. "I'll ask around."

"Thank you. I considered running an ad in the local paper, but Debra told me it helps to have someone the Amish trust intercede for a non-Amish person like myself."

"She is right. Many Amish view outsiders with suspicion. Because we seldom involve the law in our troubles, outsiders have been known to take advantage of us.

"Speaking of the law, have they found out who set the fires?" Debra asked.

Lillian shook her head. "Not yet."

"I hope they catch him. I'd like to wring the hoodlum's neck for putting my sister and all your children in danger."

"We have forgiven him," Lillian said. "None of us bears him ill will. We pray that he repents, for God is the ultimate judge of a man's soul. Someday he will meet God face-to-face and answer for his sins."

Brandon shrugged. "That is gracious of you, but I'm a man who likes to see justice done in this world as well as the next."

Debra began limping toward the school. "Don't let his bloodthirsty talk fool you. He may growl like a bear, but he's a kitten on the inside."

Brandon followed her. "I am not a kitten."

"Yes, you are," she called over her shoulder. "A spitting, fuzzy, fierce kitten."

"You got the fierce part right."

Lillian smiled at their banter. "Does your field manager have to be Amish? We have a few non-Amish farmers in the area who might be interested in working for you."

Brandon turned toward her with a sheepish grin on his face. "They wouldn't have to be Amish, but I wanted to see firsthand some of your Amish farming practices. Your friend Timothy got me to thinking about the advantages of horse drawn equipment. For one thing, soil compaction would be almost nil from the horses compared to tractors that can weigh in excess of a ton."

"That reminds me," Debra said. "I want to stop at that gift shop before we head home today. I have a friend expecting a new baby and one who just bought her first home. I wanted to get them something unique."

"Ana Bowman has some pretty baby quilts you might like. Timothy's brother Luke makes some interesting yard art. Did you notice the gourd bird feeders in the oak tree at the turn off?"

"I did. I also noticed the honor system payment box. Does it work? Do people put in the right amount or do gourds disappear without being paid for?"

"I have never heard Ana complain that she is being cheated."

Lillian followed the pair inside and waited until Debra had recovered the data she needed. As they left the building, Brandon popped open the trunk of his car. "I have a little gift for your sister."

He pulled out an aluminum folding step stool. "Is it

all right if I give this to her? I don't want to break any rules. This has wheels under the suction cups on the legs. It makes it easy to move from room to room instead of having to carry a step stool and it's still safe."

Touched by his gesture, Lillian accepted on her sister's behalf. "This is a lovely, practical gift. I'm sure she will enjoy it. Now I can put her to work dusting the tall places she hadn't been able to reach."

"Little people must adapt to the world. The world rarely adapts to us. I get a newsletter from our national association. It often reviews new devices, offers tips and gives little people a place to tell their stories. It is free. I can sign you up to get a copy if you'd like."

"I will discuss it with my parents. If they don't object, that would be great. I'll let you know."

After waving goodbye to the friendly couple, Lillian walked the two miles to her home, stopping at their neighbor Granny Weaver's to pick up Amanda. As she suspected, Amanda was delighted with her gift. She rolled it from place to place in the kitchen and down the hall to the linen closet to get clean sheets for her bed.

Lillian decided to fix a quick supper of grilled cheese sandwiches and tomato soup. Jeremiah came in just as she was heating the skillet. Amanda pushed her stepladder over to him. "Look what I have. It has wheels, but when I step on it, it stops rolling."

Jeremiah watched as she demonstrated, then looked at Lillian. "Where did this come from?"

"From Brandon Merrick, the little person professor I told you about."

"Why is he giving our sister gifts?"

Lillian buttered the slice of bread in her hand and

slipped the first sandwich in the hot skillet. "Because he is a nice fellow and he likes Amanda."

"The *Englisch* usually have a motive behind their gift giving. You'll see. He will want something from us."

She wished her brother wasn't so cynical. "He has leased Mr. Hanson's field for a test plot."

"What's he growing?"

"A new variety of corn. He's looking for someone to farm the ground and monitor the crop and he is hoping to hire an Amish fellow."

"Why one of us? So he can pay us pennies for our labor?"

"Not all *Englisch* are evil. There is good in every man. Brandon is interested in learning about Amish farming practices. Are you interested in the job or not? We could use the money."

"I'm not interested in entertaining some professor with our backward ways. We don't need money that badly."

She bit her lip to keep from arguing. Jeremiah wasn't open to reason on the subject of the *Englisch*. "Did you go through the mail today? I was hoping we'd get a letter from *Mamm*."

"I left it on the desk in the other room. *Mamm* says Uncle Albert wants *Daed* to work with him again."

She turned away from the stove. "Is he considering it?"

"He is."

"But that would mean moving the family back to Wisconsin."

"You and Amanda. I would stay here and keep running *Daed*'s business."

"I don't want to go back. I have a job. I'm needed here."

Amanda pushed her step stool up beside Lillian. "I don't want to go back, either. Granny Weaver makes me *wunderbar* cookies."

Jeremiah frowned at her. "You don't want to stay here without *Mamm* and *Daed*, do you?"

"Nee." Amanda's lower lip began to quiver. "I want them to come home."

Lillian hugged her. "They will. I'll read *Mamm*'s letter, but first let us have our supper."

After the meal, Lillian put Amanda to bed and sat down with her mother's letter. It was full of news about the community and about Uncle Albert's improving health. In the very last paragraph, she mentioned Uncle Albert's wish to have *Daed* working alongside him again and mentioned that they were considering it and praying about it.

Lillian folded the letter and slipped it back in the envelope. So her father really was considering moving the family back to Wisconsin. Would her parents allow her to remain with Jeremiah? Would she want to stay without Amanda?

Could she leave Timothy again? Her heart sank at the prospect.

On Wednesday, Hannah came home from school with a note for Timothy. Lillian wanted him to meet with Brandon Merrick on Friday after school. The note didn't say why.

Since he was on call for the fire department on Friday, he used the telephone in the community call box to let Walter know where he would be if they got called out, and then he walked to the school with jaunty steps. Any excuse to see Lillian was a good one.

Brandon and Debra were both sitting in students' desks at the front of the classroom facing Lillian's desk when he entered the building.

"Good afternoon," Timothy said, removing his hat. "You wanted to see me?"

Lillian gestured for him to join them. "Brandon has a proposal for you, and then I want your opinion about something else."

"I have plenty of opinions." He strolled to the front of the classroom, but chose not to try and fit into one the student desks. Instead, he pulled a folding chair from the rack in one corner of the room and sat down beside Brandon.

Brandon quickly explained his proposal, the type of information he would need collected and the fee he was authorized to pay. It seemed like a fair offer. Timothy had been dying to know what type of corn Brandon was developing. He would have taken the job for less.

"I accept." The two men shook hands.

Timothy looked at Lillian. "What proposal do you have for me, Lillian?"

"Not for you, for Brandon, but I want to know what you think of it."

Timothy marveled at the eagerness filling Lillian's eyes. She leaned forward and clasped her hands together. "Brandon, how would you feel about sharing your knowledge with my students? A guest speaker of sorts. The children could follow the progress of your crop, learn to compute the cost of fertilizer for each acre, identity weeds and insects and decide on the best treatments for each issue. We can do all this in a classroom setting, of course, but to have the hands-on experience in the field would be invaluable."

"Me, teaching Amish kids? Would that be allowed?" His expression showed his doubts.

Her gaze swung to Timothy. "What do you think? Would the school board approve a special guest lecturer? I think they will if I can show how much my scholars stand to gain by working with Mr. Merrick."

"He's talking about genetics, Lillian. Are you sure your church elders will allow that?" Debra voiced her doubts.

Lillian wasn't deterred. If anything, Timothy watched her grow more determined.

"We understand the benefits of good husbandry in our livestock. Leaning to raise a better corn crop is no different than learning to breed a better milk cow. Understanding the natural world and using that knowledge to our advantage isn't against the church's teachings. Timothy, what do you think?" She pinned her gaze on his again.

He hated to crush her eagerness. "I think the idea has merit, but I'm not a parent or a member of the school board. How I feel doesn't carry much weight. I can see one problem. Silas will be against it."

She sat back and crossed her arms. "I expect you are right about that."

Brandon glanced between the two of them. "Who is Silas?"

"The school board president. He doesn't care for outsiders."

"He's president for the rest of this year," Timothy added.

Lillian nodded. "That's true."

"His time on the board will be up in May. If he says

no, you can wait until you have a new president and present your idea again." It wasn't much, but it was the best he could offer.

"Why don't you run for the office?" Debra suggested.

"I have no children. Only the fathers or grandfathers of our children are allowed to hold a school board office."

"Are you saying that women aren't allowed to be on the school board?" Debra looked at him, her eyes wide with disbelief.

"Don't get on your high horse, sis," Brandon cautioned. "We're visitors to this community."

She settled back and crossed her arms. "Scratch everything I ever said about wanting to be Amish."

Timothy met Debra's eyes. "More can be done behind the scenes at home than can be done at the meeting, at least according to my mother. My brother Joshua is on the board. I'll put your idea to him, Lillian. We'll see what he thinks of it. If he favors it, you have a chance."

"*Goot.* If I can get the board to agree, will you share your time and talent with us, Brandon?" Lillian asked with a sweet smile that would have made Timothy agree to almost anything.

Brandon nodded. "When is the next school board meeting?"

Lillian glanced at the clock on the wall. "In about two hours."

The pager on his hip started beeping. He read the message and looked up to find everyone staring at him. "It's not another fire," he said quickly. "It's a call for a medical emergency, but I have to go."

He put his chair back and headed out the door to wait at the roadside for his ride. Lillian came out and stood with him. "I wish you could be at the meeting. I'd feel better knowing there was one person who understands why I want to do this."

He wanted to pull her into his arms and kiss away her worry, but he knew he shouldn't. A friend would not act that way. "You'll make them see the value in your idea."

"I hope so."

"And if they say no, you can bring it up next year."

She crossed her arms tightly over her chest. "I may not be here next year."

His heart skipped a beat. "Why do you say that?"

"*Daed* is thinking of moving the family back to Wisconsin."

"You can't go back. You have a job here. The children need you."

"My family needs me, too."

He took her by the shoulders and turned her to face him, but she kept her gaze down. Crooking a finger beneath her chin, he gently forced her to look at him. "Lillian, I don't want you to go. Say you will stay."

He held his breath as he waited for her reply.

Chapter Fourteen

"I want to stay," Lillian said softly.

"You don't know how happy it makes me to hear you say that," Timothy's smile lit up his face.

His relief drove home how unfair the situation was. She could never be the woman he needed, yet she didn't want a life without him. She needed his friendship, his humor, his understanding. Perhaps she was being selfish, but she couldn't help it. She was lonely.

The arrival of Walter put an end to the conversation. Timothy took a step back. "I've got to go."

Lillian laid a hand on his arm. "Be careful."

He patted her hand. "I will. I'll be praying for the success of your proposal, since I can't be there in person." He smiled and took off at a run toward his friend's truck and they drove off.

Brandon and Debra came out of the school. Lillian walked to their car with them. "Thank you again for agreeing to speak to my students."

Brandon nodded. "I'll be interested in how this turns out. Expect me back a week from Saturday. I want to do some soil tests before Timothy starts planting."

After they drove away, Lillian found herself with some unwelcome time on her hands. She got out a broom and began to sweep the floor, but the mundane task didn't take her mind off Timothy. How much longer could she keep her growing feelings for him hidden? Each time they were together, it became harder to pretend what she felt was friendship and not love.

She stopped sweeping as the realization hit her. She was falling in love with Timothy Bowman and she had no idea what to do about it.

Maybe a move back to Wisconsin was the answer. Except she had told Timothy the truth. She wanted to stay in Bowmans Crossing. She wanted to teach school and watch all her wonderful children grow up and someday teach their children. And she wanted to be near Timothy. Perhaps if he married someday and she knew he was happy, then she would be able to leave.

When the board finally arrived, she noticed there were more parents in attendance than usual, but the meeting itself that was basically the same as every other school board meeting she had attended since she started teaching at Ryder Hill School. The main difference this time was that Silas Mast stood up and thanked everyone for the help in repairing the school. The meeting was nearing the end when he asked if she had any requests. The monthly school board meeting was when she received her salary. She had been hoping for a raise this year, but she knew it wasn't likely. What she really needed was another teacher to help carry the load. Forty-two students were a lot to manage.

Lillian took a deep breath. "We are in need of new writing textbooks for the third-grade class. Ours are falling apart. I don't know how many times I can continue to glue them back together. And I have a new program I would like the board's permission to implement."

"Go on," Silas said.

"Brandon Merrick is the brother of the *Englisch* nurse who did our health exams and who stayed with us the day of the fire. He's a professor of agriculture at Central University. His specialty is genetic research and development of seed corn. He has a great deal of information he is willing to share about the process of producing hybrid seed corn. He has been able to lease Mr. Hanson's farm ground for a test plot. It is his hope, and mine, that he be allowed to teach the older children how to produce a hybrid seed crop by having them help with the record-keeping, detasseling and harvesting of his field. He is willing to share his knowledge for free and will even pay the children for their labor."

Silas frowned. "It sounds as if this project would have you and the children spend an unseemly amount of time with an outsider. I don't believe we need the *Englisch* instructing our children on how to grow crops when their parents and grandparents have been doing it for generations. Does this man make his living farming?"

"*Nee*, he does not. He is a teacher and researcher."

"Then he can't know our way of doing things. I grow corn as my father taught me. Corn needs clover, and clover needs corn. That will be good enough for my sons."

"But why do we plant clover one year and corn the next? Because clover replenishes the nitrogen in the soil. This is science being applied to practical matters to improve our way of life, not to detract from it. Brandon will only be at the school a few times each month."

A murmur of dissatisfaction went through the crowd. Silas shook his head. "*Nee*, I have said all I wish to say on the subject. Now, for our last bit of business, that of hiring another teacher. We haven't found anyone willing to take on the job in this district. We will keep looking. I understand that you currently have more students than most teachers, but perhaps you can have some of the older children help you with the younger ones."

"I am already doing that." Lillian struggled not to let her disappointment come through in her voice.

"I have received a few complaints of discipline problems," the bishop said, casting an apologetic glance toward Lillian.

She felt the heat rising in her cheeks as she fastened her gaze to the floor. She could hardly stand here and tell everyone in attendance that the school board president's son was the problem. Most of them knew it anyway. Abe liked to pick on the younger children, and he liked to do it when Lillian wasn't watching. She needed eyes in the back of her head, or another teacher to take over the upper grades. Apparently, that wasn't going to happen any time soon.

Joshua Bowman raised his hand. "I know someone who would make an excellent teacher. I would like to put Timothy Bowman's name up for consideration."

"You did what?" Timothy stared at Joshua in stunned shock. The men were gathered in the Bowmans' living room on Saturday evening. The women had gone to a quilting bee, leaving the men on their own. The smell of popcorn still lingered in the air, as the two brothers faced each other over the chest board.

Joshua moved his knight. "You heard me. I submitted your name as a potential teacher. The school board is coming by tomorrow evening to interview you."

Timothy sat back in his chair. "Why would you do that? I don't know the first thing about being a teacher."

Noah was slumped on the sofa with a magazine open on his lap. "There isn't much to it. You go to the schoolhouse every day, you give the *kinder* their assignments and then you grade those assignments. That's pretty much all there is to it."

Timothy rolled his eyes and shook his head. "That's what you think. I know for a fact that Lillian spends hours grading papers, assessing each child's learning potential and finding ways to help all of them reach that potential, to say nothing of the paperwork she has to keep up on."

Joshua stretched his palms out. "See, you already know a lot about being a teacher. Besides, I think you'll be good at it. And you'll get to see Lillian every day without having to make up excuses to go to school."

"I don't make up excuses. I simply think of things that other people don't."

"Look at it this way," Samuel said, "Monday through Friday, you'll have a chance to work beside Lillian. Imagine how grateful she will be that you're taking over some of her enormous workload. If you don't like the job, you don't have to do it next year."

"I can't be spared from the workshop until summer." Timothy looked to his father to support him.

Isaac stroked his beard with one hand. A sure sign he was carefully considering his words. "Actually, we will be able to spare you. I've had a letter from my brother Marvin. He wants his two oldest sons to apprentice with us."

Noah perked up. "Mark and Paul are coming to work here? Sweet!"

"I am considering it," Isaac said. "Your mother is in favor of it. With Joshua, Samuel and soon Luke out of the house, she's feeling down. She thinks having more young men in the house will cheer her up."

"Putting Mark, Paul and Noah together under one roof is a recipe for disaster." Samuel gave his little brother a hard stare."

"We got into a tiny spot of trouble once, but that was kid stuff." Noah dismissed his brother's worry with a wave of his hand.

"Joyriding and racing in a stolen buggy is hardly a tiny spot of trouble, and it happened last summer. If that buggy had belonged to anyone but Fannie Erb's father, you would have been in a *big* spot of trouble."

Noah held up both hands. "You are right. It was a foolish thing to do, but I've grown up a lot since then."

"Let us pray that Mark and Paul have, too," their father said.

Timothy paid scant attention to the rest of the conversation going on around him. The idea of working beside Lillian every day was both a good reason to take the job and the best reason to turn it down. The more time he spent with her, the harder it would be to maintain the guise of a friend when he wanted to be so much more. He looked at Joshua. "What does Lillian think of the idea?"

"She didn't say anything one way or the other. It's your move."

"But did she look pleased?"

"Surprised would be a better description."

That wasn't exactly encouraging. "What did the board say about letting Brandon Merrick teach a few classes?"

"Silas wouldn't hear of it. He doesn't want the children exposed to an outsider on a regular basis. A lot of the parents feel the same. Especially since these fires. Most people think they are the work of *Englisch* teen-age mischief-makers. I hope they are right. I don't like thinking one of our own would do such a thing."

Timothy rose and headed for the door.

"Where are you going?" Joshua asked.

"To see Lillian. I'm not going to consider the teach-ing position unless she is completely in favor of it. The last thing I want to do is make her job harder."

Timothy left the house and walked down to the barn. He selected a young mare named Snickers, led her out of her stall and harnessed her to an open cart. A short time later, he crossed the river through the covered bridge and urged the mare to a fast trot up the road.

He passed the school without stopping. At the edge of the woods that marked the start of the ridge, he slowed the horse and allowed her to climb the winding road at her own pace. The thick woods were ablaze with fall colors. Crimson, gold and brown leaves that had already fallen made a lush and colorful carpet along the edge of the road. He was grateful that Davey Mast had stopped the blaze before it destroyed the beauty of the woodlands.

At the top of the rise, he noticed a black car parked a little way back from the road. A natural clearing on the top of the ridge was a spot favored by English and Amish teenagers alike. The view of the farmland below presented a pretty picture. When the trees were leafed out in the spring, it also provided a secluded spot for young couples looking to be alone.

Timothy didn't recognize the car, but the man beside it was Davey Mast. He appeared to be arguing with Jer-emiah Keim. Jeremiah's horse and buggy stood on the far side of the car. Timothy caught only a few heated words the men exchanged before his horse took him over the rise and out of earshot. Whatever was going on, it was none of his business.

He forgot about the men when his mare reached the flat ground and picked up speed on her own. She was still fresh and happy to stretch her legs and he enjoyed the fast pace. He let her have her head until he reached Lillian's father's farm. Slowing the mare, he turned in the drive. Lillian was sitting on the front porch with Amanda on her lap. They held a children's book between them.

He pulled the horse to stop. *"Gutenowed."*

"Good evening, Timothy. What brings you here?" Lillian asked. "Would you like to come in?"

"It's too pretty an evening to spend inside. I'd rather go for an outing. Amanda, would you like to come for a ride with me?"

Amanda laughed as she pressed both hands to her mouth. Lillian whispered loudly enough for him to hear. "Timothy is asking you out on a date. Will you go?"

Amanda considered it and then looked up at Lillian. "If you come, too."

"I would be delighted to go for a drive with you. Fetch our shawls. The air will turn cool when the sun goes down."

Scrambling off her sister's lap, Amanda disappeared into the house briefly and came running back out with the shawls in her arms. Lillian fastened one around her sister's neck and then swung the other one over her own shoulders. Timothy got out of the cart to help them climb in. He started to pick up Amanda, but the child shook her head. *"Nee,* I can do it."

She went up the porch steps and grabbed a stepladder.

She returned to Timothy's side, set the ladder in place and happily climbed up to the cart seat. "See, I can do it."

"Your little sister is getting an independent streak like her big sister." He spoke in English, knowing Amanda hadn't yet learned the language.

Lillian smiled. "Brandon gave her the stepladder. She drags it all over the house and farm. It's very lightweight and it has wheels. With it, she can reach the pump handle to fill a pail with water and even gather the eggs by herself. She is having a ball."

"Brandon is a special fellow."

"He and his sister both. I didn't know outsiders could be so kind."

As they spoke, a buggy came up the lane and stopped beside them. Jeremiah nodded to Timothy. "Good day."

"Timothy invited me on a date," Amanda declared happily.

Jeremiah gave Lillian a knowing smile. "Did he, now? I'm on my way to Merle Yoder's place to give him a bid on some concrete work. I heard his dog had puppies a few weeks ago, and I thought you might want to come along to see them."

Amanda's eyes lit up. "*Ja*, I want to see the puppies." She held out her arms for Timothy to help her down. He transferred her to Jeremiah's buggy.

"You two have a nice outing." Jeremiah grinned and winked at Timothy.

"Did you get the bid on the Troyers' new farrowing house?" Lillian asked.

Timothy had heard their neighbors to the north were expanding their hog production. Jeremiah's grin vanished. "They gave it to an *Englisch* crew from Berlin. I thought the Troyers were our friends, but money speaks loudly even to the Amish," he said bitterly. He turned his horse and drove away.

Lillian started to get out, but Timothy stopped her. "It's still a nice evening for a ride. My heart was set on taking Amanda, but I reckon you will do in a pinch. Will you come with me?"

He held his breath as he waited for her answer.

Chapter Fifteen

As Timothy had hoped, Lillian grinned at his teasing tone. Her chin came up. "As my *boo-friend* has not come by, I expect an outing with you is better than sitting home alone. And it is a pretty evening."

Timothy let out the breath he was holding and eagerly climbed up beside her. Time alone with her was exactly what he wanted. He slapped the reins to get the horse moving. When they reached the highway, he stopped. "Which way should we go?"

She pointed toward the ridge. "To the top."

"To the top it is." He headed the horse back the way he had come.

"Well?" Lillian asked after a few minutes.

"Well what?" He glanced at her out of the corner of his eye.

"Don't keep me in suspense a moment longer. Are you going to take the teaching job?"

"That depends." He kept his gaze straight ahead.

"On what?"

He turned to look her full in the face. "On you."

She looked away. "I think you would make a fine teacher."

"That's not what I'm asking. Do you want me to take the job? Will working with me make you uncomfortable?"

She gave him a bright smile. Perhaps too bright. "Why would I object to working with my best friend? I can teach the first four grades and you can teach the upper grades. My workload will be cut in half. If you behave yourself and don't flirt with strange women, we'll get along fine."

"I wasn't flirting and that's beside the point. Are you sure you are okay with the idea?"

"I am. When do you start?"

"I haven't been hired yet. The school board is coming to interview me tomorrow."

"They will take you. They're desperate."

"Now, just a minute. Desperation will have nothing to do with my being hired. They will examine my many fine qualities and beg me to accept."

She chuckled. "Your lack of *demut* might be your undoing."

"I am humble."

"That is not the word I would use to describe you."

"I have my faults like everyone else, but I'm teachable. Seriously, Lillian, are you okay with this?"

"Of course I am. So please stop asking unless you want a different answer. I do thank you for seeking my opinion. It didn't count for much with our school board when I put forth my proposal."

"I'm sorry they turned down the idea of having Brandon give a few lectures. I'm certainly interested in what he has to say. I think I could learn a lot from the man."

She twisted in her seat to face him. "Timothy, that's it. That's the perfect answer. You will learn all you can from Brandon while you are working for him and then pass that information on to your students. The board can't object if you are in charge of the project. Brandon doesn't have to speak to our students. You can."

"Our students. I like the sound of that. I never considered teaching as a vocation. I always thought of it as a woman's job."

"There aren't many men teachers in our Amish schools, but their numbers are growing. I've met several of them at our annual teachers' meetings. Parents and school boards have seen the benefits of having a teacher who remains for years instead of having young women who only teach a year or two before they quit to get married."

"I'm not sure I want to do it for years. I couldn't believe Joshua submitted my name in the first place. He should have asked me first."

"Perhaps the Lord prompted your brother to suggest you. The Lord moves in mysterious ways.

"His wonders to behold," he added softly, thinking she was a wondrous person, a true gift to her students and to her friends. He was glad to be counted among those.

As the horse climbed the hill again, she began listing the things the school board might ask about and gave him an impromptu interview.

Finally, she said, "I think you will do."

"What supplies will I need if they do want me?" He wasn't sure he would get the job, but he wanted to be ready if the board said yes.

She listed things he'd already thought about like pens, markers and paper clips. A teacher was responsible for bringing his or her own supplies. At the top of the hill,

Timothy turned into the now-empty clearing and stopped the buggy. The land spread out below was a colorful patchwork of fields and woodlands laid out like a giant crazy quilt.

Lillian sighed. "I love this spot."

"So do I. I saw Jeremiah up here with Davey Mast when I came by earlier."

A frown cut a deep crease between her brows. "Are you sure?"

"*Ja.* Why?"

"Because Jeremiah told me Davey had moved to Philadelphia."

"Maybe he's back to visit some of his family and friends. Or maybe he didn't like the city and has come back for good."

"It would be wonderful if he has returned to our faith."

"I don't think that is the case. The car I saw him with was new and he was dressed fancy, not plain." Should he tell her they had been arguing? He decided against it. He wasn't certain of what he had heard and seen.

"I pray for Davey because I know Jeremiah misses his friendship."

"Will Jeremiah move back to Wisconsin with your parents?"

"I don't know. He thinks *Daed* will let him take over the construction business here and run the farm."

"But Amanda will go with them. What will you do without her?" He knew how close she was to her sister.

"Cry a lot."

He laid his hand over hers and squeezed it gently. "I know it won't be the same, but you can visit her over the summer or she can stay with you when school is out."

* * *

Lillian drew comfort from his touch and laced her fingers with his. "You are always there for me, Timothy. You know what I'm thinking or feeling better than anyone. Better than my own family."

"Don't give me too much credit."

"I don't think I give you enough credit." She looked into his hazel eyes and saw understanding and compassion, the things she loved most about him.

There was no denying it. She was in love with him. Head over heels in love in spite of her best efforts to remain simply a friend. She wanted his touch, his kisses, she wanted to be held in his arms and be cherished by him.

His grip on her hand tightened. "You are a special person, Lillian. My life would be incomplete without you in it."

Lillian closed her eyes. She didn't want to look into the chasm his words had opened between them. His life would be incomplete *with her*. He deserved a loving wife who could give him children of his own. She wouldn't take that dream from him. She cared for him too much.

Pulling her hand from his, she brushed back a stray lock of hair at her temple. "Then it's a good thing we are going to be teaching together. Imagine the fun we will have. I know you are going to love the job as much as I do and you'll see why I won't ever give it up. It's getting chilly, isn't it? I think we should head back."

"Is something wrong," he asked.

Lillian kept her gaze straight ahead. She didn't want to see disappointment in his eyes. It was bad enough that she heard it in his voice.

She had her emotions under control, but it wouldn't

take much to send her defenses crashing around her ears. "Nothing's wrong. I have enjoyed the evening, but I have work to do at home. It was nice of you to think of me and I'm very glad we will be teaching together. I promise to do everything in my power to help you."

It was a promise she intended to keep.

One week later, Timothy stood in front of the school and wondered what had possessed him to accept the job when the school board offered it. "I can't believe I'm going to do this. I'm no teacher."

"You did it for the money."

He spun around to see Lillian smiling at him. His spirits rose. "*Nee*, the salary won't make me a rich man, that's for sure, but this was a bad idea."

"So why did you accept?" She had her books clutched tightly to her chest.

"I knew you could use some help." It was true. He did want to lighten her load. More than that, he wanted to be near her. To see her smiling at him the way she was smiling now.

"I appreciate that, Timothy. Shall we go in?"

"Do I have to?"

"Well, you could stand out here the whole day. Or you could go home, but you wouldn't be much help to me either way." She started toward the door. Timothy took a deep breath and followed her.

Inside the building, he noticed someone had moved a scarred oak desk up beside hers. His desk. He really was going to go through with this. For one term. "Tell me everything I need to know before the children get here."

She started laughing. He scowled at her. "What's so funny?"

"I have been teaching for three years and I still don't know all I need to know. You will do fine."

Her belief in him bolstered his spirits enough to settle the butterflies in his stomach. "Can you at least give me some hints to get through the day?"

"Sure. Keep breathing."

"I can handle that."

"Relax. I don't plan to throw you to the wolves. I spent six weeks working with the last teacher before she left to marry. You are simply going to be helping me while you learn the ropes. Things haven't changed much since you and I sat in these desks. You already know the routine. What are some of your memories about school?"

He closed his eyes. "Getting here early enough to play ball for an inning before the bell rang. Putting my soup on the stove to stay warm until lunchtime. Copying the math assignment from the board. Saying the Lord's Prayer. Standing up front to sing poorly. I hated that. Slipping a note to Jenny Holms asking her if she would go to a singing with me when we are old enough and praying I wouldn't get caught doing it."

"You liked Jenny Holms? I never knew that. Did she ever go to a singing with you?"

"Sure."

"Who else did you walk out with?"

"Oh, I took a lot of girls home from singings in my time. During my *rumspringa*, I had a fancy open-topped buggy and a flashy fast horse. I even had a stereo installed under the dash of my ride. I rocked the whole country when I had it blaring."

"I'm shocked. Absolutely shocked. I thought you were the quiet one of the Bowman boys."

"I was. Our poor mother. You were in Wisconsin and missed all the fun here."

"So it would seem. What happened to the buggy?"

"I sold it."

"And the horse?"

"I still have her. She's not so fast these days, but she is gentle. Did you do much dating in Wisconsin?" He realized they had never talked about their years apart.

"I did my share."

"Were you ever serious about anyone?"

She sat down at her desk and propped her chin on her hand. "There was one boy. Arnold Weaver. He had red curly hair. We were in love for a few months."

"What happened?"

"I was in love with him, but it turned out that he was in love with Karen Coblentz. Happily, I realized Karen was a much better match for him. It wasn't true love for me, but it was for them. They married just before my family moved back here."

"And there was never anyone else?"

"Not to speak of. How about you? Did you ever come close to marriage?"

"I didn't. There are many fine Amish women in this community, but none of them made my heart beat faster. Maybe I'm too picky. That's what *Mamm* says. Maybe I should settle for nice and be happy."

"You shouldn't settle."

"No?"

"No. Find the one who makes your heart beat faster. She's out there."

He gazed into her beautiful green eyes. "You're right, she is."

A faint blush colored Lillian's cheeks. Timothy hoped

she knew he was talking about her. If she did, she gave
no sign of it. Was he mistaken in thinking she returned
his affection?

Was friendship all she wanted from him?

The first student came bursting in the door. It was
Carl Mast. "Teacher, look what I made for you."

He proudly handed Lillian a drawing of stick figures gathered around a campfire. One of the figures
had smoke circling around his head. "This is my family.
That's Davey because he smokes now and *Daed* doesn't
like it. *Daed* won't talk to him, but Davey says it's okay
if I do. Is it okay, Teacher?"

Lillian knelt to be on Carl's level. "It is fine for you to
talk to Davey. You are not yet baptized and the rules on
shunning don't apply to you. I'm sorry your father won't
speak to him. He wants Davey to come back to the church.
We all pray for that, but each man must find his own way
to God. Maybe that's what Davey is doing."

She glanced at Timothy and caught his nod. He agreed
with her attempt to comfort the child and explain a difficult subject. Religion was not part of their school curriculum. That was the sacred duty of parents and church
ministers. She looked at the picture and then at Carl. "I
want you to go hang this with the other art work. You
did a fine job."

"Danki." He smiled a gap-toothed grin, went to the
corkboard behind her desk and pinned it up.

She looked at Timothy. "Would you erase the board
and put up the new arithmetic assignment? I've written
them out in the red notebook on my desk."

"Of course. Carl, would you like to help me?"

"Sure." The boy scampered to his side and began

making big sweeps with the eraser as high as he could reach.

As the day went on, Lillian knew the board had made a wise decision when they hired Timothy. He moved among the children offering help, encouragement and praise. Twice he stepped behind Abe and stopped the boy from passing a note. He whispered something in the boy's ear that she didn't hear, but it was effective. Abe was as good as gold the rest of the day.

At recess, he joined the older children in a ball game and earned huge marks for his ability to hit the ball over the outfield fence. As the last student went out the door at the end of the day, Timothy sank into his chair and looked at her. "This isn't the job for me."

"Are you going to quit?" Lillian's stunned expression told Timothy she had taken him seriously.

"I have said I would teach for one term. I'm not going to break my word, but I feel sorry for the *kinder* that will have to put up with me until summer."

"You didn't do so badly." She sat in the student desk next to him.

"I didn't do that well. There has to be someone better out there."

"They did not step forward when the position was opened. You're going to do fine. Give yourself a chance."

"All of your students can conjugate verbs better than I can. I felt foolish trying to explain something I don't understand."

"Now you know how I feel about teaching science. I am woefully inadequate in that field, but I can conjugate with the best of them. Present tense. I see. You see. He sees. We see. You see. They see."

"Right. So explain to me why everyone can see, but he/she/it sees."

"English is a complicated language."

"It is. It was. It will be."

She smiled at him. "Very good."

"Only because Susan Yoder did it for me."

"She'll make a fine teacher someday, and so will you."

"Can we go over the lesson plans for tomorrow? I don't want to feel so flat-footed in front of the children again."

"Of course. Pull your chair over here." She scooted her chair to the end of her desk to make room for him.

"How long did it take you to learn all this?" he asked.

"I haven't learned it all. I'm still discovering better ways to teach. I think the most frustrating thing about English is that so many words don't sound like they look. I think I am teaching the right way to say a word only to find out later that I have been mispronouncing something for ages."

"High German is much more straightforward," he said.

"I agree."

"Have you noticed how much trouble Hannah has reading aloud?" he asked.

"I've been working with her, but I can't seem to find the key that will boost her confidence."

"I've read that some children do better at reading to their pets than reading to other people. Have you heard of that?"

"I have. Do you think we should let Bella come to school?"

"It's worth a try, isn't it?"

"Sure."

She flipped open a ledger and found tomorrow's date. "Your upper grades will study cell structure and write an essay on the subject at the end of the week."

"At least that's something I can handle."

"I'm glad, because that is something that completely escapes my understanding. Why don't we leak away if we are 90 percent water? What makes all our cells stick together in the same fashion every day?"

"We don't leak because of cell membranes. They keep the fluids inside."

She started chuckling. "What's so funny?" he demanded.

"Do you realize how well suited to this job we would be if we could somehow combine us into one new and improved teacher?"

"I prefer to think we complement each other. Where I lack, you excel and vice versa."

"It does seem that way." Her voice was little more than a whisper.

"We make a good team," he said softly. He fought down the urge to reach out and touch her face.

"Yes, we do." She sounded almost breathless now.

If he leaned in a little more, he could kiss her. Would she let him?

She pulled back and looked away. "That's why you can't quit. I need your help.

"I won't quit. Not until the school board can find someone to replace me."

She stood and gathered her books into her arms, holding them close to her chest. "I hope that takes a very long time. I knew I would enjoy working with you, but I must get home. Do you need a textbook to read up on your subjects for tomorrow?"

"That would be great."

She moved across the room to the shelves that held the school's library books. After scanning the contents, she selected a volume and held it toward him. "I have found this book to be the most helpful with science. It has some wonderful illustrations."

Timothy tipped his head to the side at a new sound. "Do I hear a siren?"

Lillian listened. "I hear it, too. Not again."

They went outside and turned in every direction. He couldn't see any sign of smoke.

"Maybe it's a medical call," Timothy said.

Somehow he knew in his heart it wasn't. As they stood in front of the school, the siren grew louder until the fire engine rounded the curve, heading toward the ridge. Luke leaned out the passenger's side and shouted, "Weaver's farm. Get on the next truck."

Lillian clutched Timothy's arm. "Amanda is spending the day with Granny Weaver. She lives in the *daadi* house at the Weaver place."

"We'll take care of her. Don't worry." He hoped it wasn't an empty promise. The second, smaller fire truck came around the bend. It stopped to let him get on and then roared away.

Looking back, he saw Lillian running toward home.

Chapter Sixteen

Everyone in the Amish school was subdued the next morning, including the teachers. Lillian knew all the children had heard about the fire. Everyone was thankful there had been no loss of life. All fifty pigs had been saved, but the new hog house under construction had been a total loss. Lillian could see the unease on the young faces of those looking to her for comfort and guidance, and she wasn't sure how to help them.

Amanda had refused to go to Granny Weaver's home that morning. She sat at a small student desk beside Lillian's large one. She was quietly coloring in one of her books, but Lillian noticed every page had been scribbled over with red.

Lillian sent Timothy a silent plea for help. She had already opened the morning with a Bible verse, the twenty-third Psalm, and the children had recited the Lord's Prayer. Normally, she would have the children come up to sing, but today did not seem normal.

Timothy moved his chair from his desk and parked it at the top of the aisle between the rows of children. "Many of you know that I serve as a volunteer fireman. I helped put out the fire last night. I was wondering if any of you have questions that I might be able to answer."

Susan Yoder tentatively raised her hand. He motioned to her. She rose to her feet. "My *daed* says the fire was started on purpose by an *Englisch* fellow riding a four-wheeler. Is that who did it?"

"No one saw who started the fire. Granny Weaver did see a fellow on a four-wheeler about twenty minutes before she noticed the smoke. It could've been that man. But maybe he was just out having a good time and had nothing to do with the fire."

Hannah stood up. Bella, her yellow Lab, lay quietly beside her chair. "I wish you and my *daed* wouldn't go to the fires anymore. I heard my *mamm* say it's getting too dangerous."

"A fire is a dangerous thing. But your *daed* and I and all the other firemen are very careful. We don't want anyone to get hurt."

"Why do the *Englisch* hate us?" Abe asked.

"The *Englisch* do not hate us," Lillian replied.

"Then why are they starting all these fires?" Gabriel demanded.

"My *mamm* says she isn't going to sell any more quilts to them," little Marietta Yoder said with a fierce scowl on her face. Her older sister, Susan, hushed her.

Timothy laced his fingers together and leaned forward with his elbows on his knees. "We must not hold a grudge or blame everyone for the acts of one or two people,"

"He is right." Lillian moved to stand beside him. "We must forgive those that trespass against us. Isn't that what we say when we repeat the Lord's Prayer? Forgive us our trespasses as we forgive those who trespass against us. We do not punish or condemn. That is not our way."

"What should we do?" Susan asked.

"We must do as we have always done. Take care of one another and trust the Lord to guide and protect us. We must be kind. We must be gentle in the way we live and humble before God. Our Lord has a greater purpose for each one of us. If we are quiet in our hearts, we can hear His will and obey."

Timothy stood up. "All right, fourth-grade class, I need you to take out your spelling workbooks. We are having a pop quiz."

Lillian heard a small groan from the class but decided to ignore it. She beckoned to Susan Yoder. "For reading today, I want each of the second graders to go to the chair I have set up in the back corner, and each of them is to spend fifteen minutes reading to Bella."

"To the dog?" Susan looked as if she hadn't heard correctly.

"To the dog. The students are to raise their hand if they don't know a word. Otherwise, they are simply to read aloud. They may choose any book they would like."

"Why?"

"It's an experiment."

"It's kind of silly, but okay. Is the dog going to be tested over what she has heard?"

Lillian cupped a hand over her chin as if she were considering the idea. After a few seconds, she smiled and shook her head.

Timothy winked at Lillian before he turned to Susan. "I'm afraid the dog would score higher than the rest of us, and that wouldn't look good on our year-end report."

Lillian burst out laughing, and Timothy joined in. Susan walked away shaking her head at their foolishness.

Over the next two weeks, Timothy found his footing in his new job and began to enjoy it. Each hurdle that one of his students overcame filled him with joy. Abe had stopped pestering the younger children. Once Timothy realized Abe was bored with schoolwork that was too easy for him, he started bringing him harder and harder assignments. He looked forward to the spring when he and the upper-grade boys would be doing real-life problem-solving for Brandon's project.

Often during the day, Timothy would catch Lillian watching him with a tiny smile on her face that told him she was pleased with his progress. Although he once thought he would be able to spend a lot of time with her, forty-two students turned out to be incredibly efficient chaperones. At best, he and Lillian had a few minutes before the students arrived and a few minutes after they left to enjoy each other's company. Even that time was often spent discussing new lesson plans and potential curriculum changes for the coming year. She had to hurry home to take care of Amanda and run her home, while he had to put in several hours in his father's workshop.

His younger cousins Mark and Paul Bowman had arrived the previous weekend. While they didn't have a great deal of skill as woodworkers, they had a lot of enthusiasm.

Like everyone else, Timothy and his family were on edge wondering when and who the arsonist would target next. Distrust of their *Englisch* neighbor's was growing within the community. The Hansons had been the only non-Amish family targeted. The investigation by the fire marshal was ongoing, but he divulged little or no information, further frustrating the Amish.

On the last Friday of the month, Timothy and Lillian walked outside after the children had been dismissed. The air held a decided chill. Winter was tapping at the door.

The playground was empty. The students had gone. Timothy breathed in the clean, crisp air and smiled. It had been a wonderful week. Wonderful because he had been able to share it with Lillian.

She pulled her shawl tight across her chest. "Don't you love how quiet it is when they aren't here?"

"Actually, I kind of miss the noise."

Looking over the schoolyard, he noticed a doll that had been forgotten beside the swing set. Walking over, he picked it up and brushed the dirt from the little black apron. "I see one of our scholars couldn't bear to leave school."

Lillian took it from him. "This belongs to Marietta. She'll be missing it soon. She rarely goes anywhere without it. I'll drop it by her house on my way home."

Lillian would do anything for her students. "I see why you do it. I see why you say you love this job. You are so good at it."

She poked him in the chest. "So are you. Hannah has been struggling to read for ages. She was embarrassed to read aloud in front of the other students. Having her read to Bella was the perfect answer."

"It was only something I read. I wasn't sure it would work."

"Bella makes a wonderful teacher's helper. Devoted, uncritical of Hannah's slow and painful progress. She simply wants to have Hannah and the others beside her. It is the dog's acceptance of their less than perfect attempts that give them the courage to try more."

"We should ask the school board to give Bella a salary," he said with a chuckle.

"You can give the dog the credit if you want, but you are the one who helped Hannah succeed. I saw the light in her eyes when she finished her first book. She was so excited."

"I saw it, too," he admitted.

Lillian took a seat on the swing, pushed back and began to swing to and fro. "That is exactly why I love this profession. Every child has such bright potential. To see them uncover that potential is a gift."

Timothy stepped behind her and gave her a gentle push. "I wonder if you know how much your eyes light up when you talk about these children."

Lillian smiled. "I know pride is a sin, but I am proud of the children and all they accomplish."

"It is not a sin to take pride in what others have accomplished. Only to take pride in what we believe we have achieved, when God is the giver of every gift. I'm amazed at what you and the children have taught me. The Lord has blessed me with many gifts, Lillian, but chief among them is the friendship of an honorable woman."

She felt the heat rise in her cheeks. "*Danki*. Your friendship is a gift to me, too. What interesting thing do you have planned for your seventh and eighth graders next week?" she asked to steer the conversation away from personal things.

"For my history class, I thought we would build several Native American structures, since we're studying the tribes of the Eastern states first. By the end of the week, we will be studying the Plains Indians and the tribes of the desert Southwest. Since we don't have any cliffs that we can carve into homes, I thought I would have them build a tipi and a wigwam. Then I think I'll have them write an essay on comparisons using the structures for our English lesson." He gave her a shove, sending her swinging higher.

"Killing two birds with one stone, very *goot*. Turning your history lesson into an English lesson is smart, and I'm sure the children will enjoy it."

"I expect I will have to supply the poles and saplings."

"At least you don't have to kill a buffalo for the hide."

"*Nee*, I think a large tarp will serve the same purpose."

She leaned backward in the swing so that she could see him. "This is fun, isn't it?"

"Playing on the swings?"

"*Nee*, talking about the children, about their problems and their successes. Sharing what we would like them to learn. It's fulfilling." She hadn't realized how lonely it had been being the only teacher. Now that she had Timothy to share her joys and sorrows, it made her happiness complete.

He stopped her and twisted the chains around so that she was facing him. "I do like sharing my days with you. These past two weeks, I have been happier than I've ever been in my life, and it's all because of you."

She knew that he was going to kiss her. The rational part of her mind said all she had to do was turn her face aside. The lonely womanly part of her mind made her lift her face to him and close her eyes.

The touch of his lips was oh so gentle. He pulled

back. She opened her eyes. He was waiting for her protest. She didn't want to object. All she wanted was to feel the touch of his lips again. And that was foolishness.

She slipped out of the swing and stood. He let go of the chains and cupped her face in his hands. "You are so beautiful."

Before she could reply, he was kissing her again. Somehow her arms found their way to his shoulders and then around his neck as he pulled her close and deepened the kiss. Nothing had ever felt as wonderful as being held in his embrace. She leaned closer and the world slipped away leaving them the only two creatures in the universe, bound together by a newfound passion.

His lips were firm but gentle as he brushed the corner of her mouth. She tipped her head slightly offering him her silent consent. He took advantage of her willingness. His mouth moved back to hers and he deepened the kiss. It was more wonderful than she had imagined. Her heart galloped in her chest as her breath came in short bursts. She gripped his shoulders to steady herself and kissed him back.

A few long wonderful seconds later, he pulled away. She opened her eyes to stare up at him. His face mirrored her wonderment. She didn't know how to react or what to say.

Regret slowly filled eyes. "I'm sorry, Lillian. I shouldn't have done that."

She pressed her hand to her lips. They still tingled from his touch. There was no going back to the way things were before. "Don't be sorry."

"I never meant for this to happen."

"I know, but it has. Now we have to face the fact that we are only human."

"I care for you. As a friend and as a woman."

"Then as my friend, I'm going to ask you to forget that this happened."

"I don't think I can."

She touched her fingers to his lips. "You must. There is no future for us on this path."

"How can you say that?"

She stepped away from him. "I say it because it is the truth. You're a fine man. The woman who wins your heart will be blessed above all others. My heart belongs to the children, Timothy. I won't give them up. There can't be a repeat of this. Perhaps you should go now."

She could see he wanted to say more, but in the end, he simply nodded.

"All right. I'm sorry." He turned and walked away.

Lillian watched him until he was out of sight around the bend in the road. Then she sank to her knees as silent tears marked their paths down her cheeks.

Timothy walked home with his emotions in turmoil. He didn't regret kissing Lillian, but it had been a mistake. He had asked her to choose between him and the thing she loved. She cared deeply for him, her kiss told him that, but she wasn't going to give up teaching.

He reached the bridge and started across the river using the pedestrian walkway that had been built alongside the covered bridge. Halfway across, he stopped and rested his arms on the railing as he stared down into the churning waters. He'd been a fool, but at least he didn't have to hide his feelings any longer.

"I hope you aren't planning to jump."

He looked up to see Joshua coming toward him. "I'm

not. I don't see how getting cold and wet will improve my outlook."

"What's wrong?" Joshua stopped beside him.

Timothy continued staring at the water. "I kissed Lillian."

"I take it things didn't go well afterward."

"Not exactly. She likes me a lot, but she won't give up teaching."

"That's tough. What are you going to do about it? I'd sure hate to see you quit. Hannah speaks very highly of you. She says Abe Mast doesn't tease her anymore because you won't let him."

"I'm glad I made one person happy."

"Did you tell Lillian she doesn't have to make a decision right away? That you would wait for her?"

"I didn't get a chance to say much, but I don't want to wait."

"Isn't she worth it?"

"She is worth it. Do you think I've ruined my chances with her?"

"No one but Lillian can answer that."

"What do you think I should do?"

When she got home that evening, Lillian washed her face at the outside pump, scrubbing away the last traces of her tears. She didn't expect Jeremiah to notice she had been crying, but she didn't want to explain if he did. Entering the house, she hung her bonnet and shawl from a peg by the front door. She noticed that Amanda's shawl was missing.

Turning around, she saw Amanda running in from the other room to greet her. Jeremiah came to the door of the living room. "You're kind of late getting home tonight."

"I had a lot to do at school." She looked down at Amanda. "Where have you left your cloak this time?"

Amanda scrunched up her face as she tried to remember. "I think I left it in Jeremiah's buggy. We went to see the puppies again and we had supper with the Weaver family. I might get a puppy of my own when they are old enough. Shall I go get my cloak?"

Lillian shook her head. "Go get ready for bed and say your prayers. I will find it in the morning."

Jeremiah said, "Mrs. Weaver sent some supper home with us. It's in the oven if you want it."

"*Danki*. How is the job going?" He had won the bid on their construction project.

"It's good. I might have another job lined up when I'm done with this one."

"You're working so hard. *Daed* will be pleased with you. Was there any mail?"

He gestured toward the counter. "A letter from *Mamm*. I'll let you read it. I'm going to turn in."

"Good night."

Lillian pulled her supper out of the stove, but found she wasn't hungry. She ate a few bites and put the rest away. She wasn't sleepy; far from it. She needed something to take her mind off Timothy's kisses. His wonderful, wonderful kisses. Now that she knew what she was giving up, it was even harder to think about staying friends.

She opened her mother's letter and read through the three pages quickly. *Onkel* Albert continued to improve, and her father now planned to return to Wisconsin permanently. They would be home in two weeks to pack up and arrange the move. There were two openings for teachers in the area if Lillian decided she didn't want to stay in Bowmans Crossing but wanted to return to Wisconsin with her parents and Amanda. The decision wasn't as simple as it had seemed before Timothy kissed her.

Restless, and undecided, she pulled on her shawl and opened the door, hoping a short walk would bring some peace of mind. Her brother had parked the buggy in its usual place beside the barn. Taking a flashlight from the kitchen drawer, Lillian went to get her sister's cloak.

The night air had a distinct chill to it and she wished she had taken the time to put on her heavier cloak. She hurried across the yard and opened the buggy door. She shone the light on the front seat, but it was empty. Amanda had probably left her shawl at the Weaver Farm. She just hoped it hadn't been left with the puppies.

She pulled open the back door, swept her light across the interior and caught sight of a small amount of fringe sticking out from under the seat. She reached over and pulled the garment free. As she did, a blue metal canister rolled out with it. Lillian realized she was looking at a propane tank. Picking it up, she could tell it was full by the weight. The cool metal tank was perfectly harmless by itself. It was only when it was attached to a device made especially for it, such as a lantern, a flame-spreading head or a camp stove, that the gas inside was released and could be ignited.

She turned the beam of her light under the seat and pulled out two more canisters. Why would her brother have so many of these small bottles? Jeremiah had never cared for campouts and she'd never seen him with a propane lantern. He preferred battery-operated torches like the one she held.

A cold breeze sent a sudden shiver down her spine.

Were these the same kinds of canisters the arsonist had used to start his fires?

Timothy would know. Should she tell him? What if her brother had them for an innocent purpose and he was unjustly arrested because of her? It had happened to Timothy's brother. She was duty-bound to protect Jeremiah until she was absolutely sure of his guilt.

The simple thing to do was to ask Jeremiah why he had them, but she couldn't. How could she admit she suspected her own brother had committed these crimes?

Lillian bundled the canisters together in Amanda's shawl and carried them into the house. Both Amanda and Jeremiah had gone to bed. In her room, she found a box and laid the canisters in it. Glancing around, she realized it would be easy for Jeremiah to find them if he searched the house. She needed a better hiding place. Would he think to search the school? Maybe, but it was better than having them where he might easily find them.

Grabbing her heavy cloak, she went out the door and walked silently through the night until she reached the school. She placed the box in the bottom drawer of a filing cabinet and locked the drawer. On Monday, she would ask Timothy what she should do. He was the one person she knew she could trust.

Chapter Seventeen

Early on Saturday morning, Timothy hitched up his buggy and drove to the home of Bishop Beachy. He needed advice. There had to be a way to let Lillian keep teaching and for them to be together. The bishop came out of the house when Timothy arrived.

Lines of worry sat heavily on the bishop's face, but he managed a smile. "Good Morning, Brother Timothy. What brings you out this way?"

"I am in need of your counsel."

"Well, then, come in. What is troubling you?" The bishop opened the door of his house and Timothy stepped into the kitchen that smelled of dough and fresh-baked bread.

The bishop's wife looked up with a bright smile. "Hello, Timothy. I'm afraid you caught me making bread. I'm covered in flour."

"Don't mind me. *Mamm* is making bread this morning, too.

"It's all right, dear," the bishop said. "Timothy and I will be in my office."

"Shall I bring you some coffee?" she offered, dusting her hands on her apron.

"Nothing for me, *danki*," Timothy said.

"Don't interrupt your work. We'll be fine." The bishop led the way to the rear of the house and a small bedroom that now served as his cluttered workspace. He moved some books from a chair and gestured to Timothy. "Sit down. How can I help you?"

"You know that Lillian and I are both teaching at the school."

"*Ja*. How is that working out for you?"

"Fine. I love it. Never in my wildest dreams would I have considered being a teacher, but now I can't imagine doing anything else."

"I'm happy to hear that. The Lord moves in mysterious ways, does He not? So, what is the problem?"

"Lillian loves teaching, too. As much as I do, or more."

"We are blessed to have two people so dedicated to our children."

"I want to ask Lillian to marry me."

"Oh, I see. That's a big step. Are you sure this is what God wants for you?"

"I hope it is. I've prayed about it, but I know Lillian doesn't want to give up teaching. Is there a reason she can't teach after we are married?"

"Being a wife and a mother is a sacred duty that must come before any job, Timothy. I'm sure you understand that."

"I do, but couldn't she continue to teach until our first babe arrives?"

"This is an unusual request. I, too, must pray about it."

Timothy hid his disappointment. He wanted an answer today.

"Will it be awkward for the two of you to continue to work together?" the bishop asked.

Timothy shook his head. "The children take all our time during school hours. They have our full attention. I don't let my feelings for Lillian interfere with my work."

"How do you think the *kinder* would feel knowing the two of you were wed?"

"I think they would accept it. Many married couples work together. Emma and Luke will work together in her store. Rebecca helps Samuel with record-keeping and orders for the business. Every wife is a helpmate to her husband."

"What you say is true. If the school board has no objections, I can offer none."

Timothy left the bishop's home feeling more hopeful. If he could convince Lillian he was willing to have a long engagement and that she could work after their marriage until their own children came along, she might find it acceptable. There was only one flaw in his plan. Lillian hadn't said that she loved him.

Timothy returned home and stopped by the woodworking building to pick up the pager. It was his day to be on call. After that, he hitched up a team to the planter. As he drove the horses across the bridge, he saw Brandon and Debra waiting for him at the edge of the field.

"Your horses are so pretty." Debra immediately went to the head of the team. The big gray Percherons lowered their heads for some attention.

Brandon stood at his vehicle with an array of soil testing chemicals spread out on the hood. "I'm almost finished."

"Do you have the seed you wish to plant?"

"In the trunk."

Timothy pulled out the bags, cut them open and began filling his planter. "How many pounds and what depth do you want?"

He and Brandon discussed the best planting strategies and then Timothy made a single round of the field. Brandon analyzed the planting depth and seed thickness and gave Timothy the thumbs-up sign. After planting half the field, Timothy pulled the team to a stop again when Brandon walked out to meet him. "Can I ride along with you?" he asked.

"Would you like to drive them?" Timothy offered.

"I'd love to." Brandon climbed into the seat with Timothy's help. Standing behind him, Timothy showed him how to hold the reins and what commands to give the horse.

Debra rushed up with her cell phone out. "I have to have a picture of this."

Timothy held a hand in front of his face palm out. "No pictures of me, please."

She looked mortified. "I'm sorry. I forgot. I'll delete this one."

He smiled. "I appreciate that. Let me step away so you can get a good picture of your brother."

He did and she took a couple of shots before putting her phone away. After that, he made several rounds of the field with Brandon's help and then let him off. Debra declined to ride. Each time he passed by the school, Timothy's gaze was drawn to the swing set beside it. He'd never again look at it without remembering that was where he had kissed Lillian. He half hoped she would come by to visit with Debra and Brandon, but she didn't. Was he the reason? Was she avoiding him now?

A little after noon, his mother and Mary came to the field with a picnic hamper. He stopped and enjoyed a hearty ham sandwich and homemade pickles for lunch. Debra had her first whoopee pie and couldn't stop raving about it. When lunch was over, she followed the women back to the house to do some shopping in his mother's gift shop.

It was growing late by the time he finished planting the large field. He stopped the team by the car where Brandon and Debra were waiting for him. "That's it," he said.

"Now all we need is a little rain," Brandon said with a smile.

Timothy wiped the sweat from his brow with the back of his sleeve. "Did you find something at the gift shop?"

"I did. Two wonderful baby quilts, several jars of homemade jam and two cute gourd birdhouses."

"I'll tell my brother Luke that you like them."

Debra sniffed the air. "Do I smell smoke?"

Timothy scanned the area. "You may be smelling the burned-out trees by the river."

"No, she's right. I smell smoke, too," Brandon said with a frown.

A second later, Timothy's pager went off. He read the message, raised the planter out of the dirt and sent his team galloping for home.

In the early-morning hours, the only wall left standing still bore traces of faint blue lettering, but the words were illegible. Lillian knew it once read Bowmans Crossing Amish-Made Gifts and Furniture. Timothy's mother's gift shop lay in ruins. Sadly, three other fires had been set in the night. Silas Mast's dairy barn was gone and thirty head of cattle had perished in the flames. Two other Amish barns had been heavily damaged. It had taken eight fire companies from the surrounding counties to control the blazes.

Emma, Mary and Rebecca were weeping openly. Joshua put his arm around his wife. "I painted that sign when I was a kid and I painted it again after I got out of prison. I reckon I can make another."

"It was too fancy anyway," Isaac said, wiping his hand across his sweaty and smoke-stained brow.

"The bishop never objected." Dry-eyed, Ana stood beside Isaac with her hands on her hips.

Isaac nudged her with his elbow. "Because he has always had a soft spot for you."

They shared a tender smile.

Lillian saw Timothy among the firemen raking through the debris and dousing embers. She longed to comfort him, but had to wait quietly until his work was done. She noticed Debra and Brandon at the edge of a group of onlookers and went over to them. Debra saw her and came to put her arms around Lillian. "This is terrible. What kind of monster does this to such peaceful people?"

"We must forgive him." Lillian gave lip service to her belief, but letting go of the anger in her heart was harder.

Brandon patted his sister on the shoulder. "What are these people going to do now?"

"Help each other rebuild," Lillian said, wondering how that was going to be possible. Everyone in the community had already given what assistance they could afford to the earlier victims.

Debra turned pleading eyes to her brother. "Brandon, we have to do something."

"We will, sis."

The fire chief came up to Isaac. "I'm afraid it looks like arson. The burn pattern matches the others. The flames were shooting up the outside of the building. It didn't start inside. We'll send pieces of wood to the lab for analysis, but I'm sure they are going to tell us it was soaked with gasoline."

"Did you find another propane bottle?"

"No, not yet," the chief admitted. "We'll do a more thorough search when the debris cools enough to let our arson squad inside. In the meantime, it's off-limits to everyone."

He turned and spoke to the crowd of onlookers. "I want everyone to go home now."

Someone shouted from the back, "Why haven't you caught this fellow? All our business and homes are at risk."

Sheriff Bradley moved to stand beside Chief Swanson. "We are working hard to find out who is behind this, but we need everyone's help. Be aware of what is going on around you. Don't be afraid to call 9-1-1 if you see something suspicious. We will check it out. If it's nothing, good. If it helps break this case, better. Now please go home."

The group reluctantly began to disperse. Timothy along with Luke came to stand beside their parents. They looked bone-tired. Lillian resisted the urge to put her arm around Timothy and offer him support. He caught sight of her, nodded and walked over. Her heart did a funny little flip as their eyes met. She was well and truly smitten.

He wiped his brow with his shirtsleeve. "I'm off duty now. I'd like to talk to you if you have some time."

"Wouldn't you like to get some rest first?"

"*Nee*, I'll wash off the grime and meet you out back of the house in *Mamm*'s garden if you can stay awhile longer."

"Are you sure it can't wait?"

"Please, humor me."

"Okay." She wasn't sure which she wanted more. A repeat of yesterday's kisses or for him to tell her they would simply be friends again.

Timothy prayed he was doing the right thing as he left the house, his hair still wet from his shower. Lillian was seated on a lattice bench beside his mother's rosebush. He took a seat beside her and took one of her hands between his own. "I have something important to say to you."

"You look so serious. What's wrong?"

"Nothing is wrong. I hope what I have to say will make you happy. I spoke with the bishop yesterday. I wanted to speak to him before I spoke with you. I know you believe you will have to give up teaching if you marry, but that isn't the case. I didn't want to say anything until I was sure."

"No, Timothy. Don't." She turned her face away from him.

He cupped her cheek. "Don't what? Don't tell you how much you mean to me? Don't tell you how happy I am when I am near you? I can't keep these things a secret any longer. I love you, Lillian. As a friend, yes, but also as the woman who holds my heart in the palm of her hand. I want you to be my wife. I want the right to hold you in my arms. I want to grow old beside you. Tell me that you love me, too. I long to hear those words from your lips."

She closed her eyes and he knew a moment of gut-wrenching fear. What if she didn't love him? How could he go on?

She pressed her hand over his where it rested on her cheek. "You don't know how hard this is."

He steeled himself to hear her rejection. "If you don't feel as I do, I understand."

Please, God, let her love me.

"Before you answer me, Lillian, let me tell you what the bishop said. I asked him if we could go on teaching together as husband and wife. He said that it would be acceptable if the school board agrees. Do you understand what I'm saying? You don't have to give up teaching. Not for a while anyway. Not until the Lord blesses us with children of our own. I can endure a long engagement if it means you will be mine in the end. Will you marry me? I love you more than life itself."

Lillian could barely see his face through her tears. She moved her hand to cup his cheek. "I know how important having children is to you, Timothy. I know you have dreams of a big family."

"I do want a big family, but more than that, I want you to be the mother of my children."

"And for that reason, I must tell you that I can't marry you." Her voice cracked as did her heart. She hated hurting him this way.

Disbelief filled his eyes. "You care for me. I know you do. I feel it in your touch. I see it when you look at me. I hear it in your laughter. You love me. I know you do."

"I do love you, Timothy."

"Then I don't understand."

"It is because I love you that I will never marry you. This is my burden, and I must carry it alone. I'm barren, Timothy. I can never have children."

He frowned. "How can you know this?"

"Shortly after my family moved to Wisconsin, I became ill. I had developed a rare form of cancer. The surgery to remove it saved my life, but it left me unable to have children. I'm sorry, Timothy. I won't marry you or anyone."

It was a shock to him. Lillian saw it on his face and wished she could have spared him this pain. She couldn't bear his look of sorrow a moment longer. "I have to go now."

She rose to her feet, and he didn't try to stop her. She was thankful for that. She didn't want him to see her heart was breaking, too.

Timothy remained on the bench in the garden at the back of the house overlooking the river. The morning air held the scents of his mother's roses and the sweet autumn clematis that climbed the trellis against the wall. The river was a wide swath of dark water traveling endlessly along. The surface looked calm, but he knew there were eddies and currents that swirled beneath the surface much like the turbulent emotions that ran ceaselessly through his brain.

"What is troubling you, my son?"

Timothy looked up to find his father standing beside him. He hadn't heard his approach. For a second, Timothy was tempted to deny he was troubled, but the words stuck in his throat. His father sat down. "This is a good thinking spot. I have always liked watching the river, don't you?"

"I do, too."

"I often sit here when I need to pray about something. I like to think I'm talking to the good Lord as a friend when I sit here in your mother's garden. Am I interrupting your prayers?"

"*Nee*, I wasn't praying."

"Should you be?"

"I would if I knew what to pray for." He met his father's gaze. "I asked Lillian to marry me."

"Did you, now? Not much of a surprise in that. The two of you seem made for each other."

Timothy leaned forward with his elbows propped on his knees. "I thought so, too. She turned me down."

"I'm sorry to hear that. It may not be any of my business, but did she give you a reason?"

"She said it would be unfair to me."

"Because her heart lies elsewhere?"

"*Nee*, she says she loves me, but won't wed me because she can't have children. She doesn't want to bind me to a barren wife for all my life."

His father stroked his long beard. "I see. She is certain of her condition?"

"She is. The doctors she saw in Wisconsin told her she would never have a child."

His father was silent for a long time. Then he said, "Children are among God's greatest gift to us. Knowing that I have sons to carry on after me gives me great comfort. I know your mother will never be alone or in need should something happen to me."

Timothy looked at his father. "My whole life I wanted to be as good a father as you have been to me."

"That is fine praise, but being a father has not always been easy. My sons are so different from each other that I sometimes used to wonder if the midwife slipped me a cowbird egg or two. Happily, I have come to see your mother and me in all of you. You take after your mother the most. You are tenderhearted and yet sensible. You care for the land and the business I have built, but you care more for the people around you. Do you love Lillian?"

"With all my heart."

"I thought as much. Do you believe she is the woman chosen by God to be your life mate?"

"I did. I don't know what to believe now. How can I see Lillian every day and know she will never be mine? I'm not strong enough, *Daed*. I had such dreams for us. I don't know how to let those go."

"Do you wish to marry her in spite of what she has told you?"

"That's just it. I'm not sure. I love her, but I want a family."

"And what is a family?"

His father's question puzzled Timothy. "Children and a wife."

"Your children?"

"Ja."

"Do you love Hannah?"

Timothy frowned at the sudden change of topic. "Of course I do."

"Joshua loves Hannah with all his heart. I love her, too, as does your mother. We all love that child, but she is no blood relation to us. Yet our family would be incomplete without her."

Hannah had been four years old when Joshua met

Mary. Joshua often said he fell in love with Hannah first and had to marry Mary in order to keep the child.

Timothy gazed out at the river again. If only the Lord would send him a sign. Something to help him know what to do. "Would you have married Mother had you known she couldn't give you sons?"

"I married your mother because God chose her to be my better half, for now and forever. There was no guarantee of children in that bargain."

"Yet you both hoped and prayed for children."

"We did pray for strong sons, and the Lord heard us. Telling a man to give up his hopes and dreams of having a family one day is a difficult thing. I cannot tell you what to do. You must decide."

The problem was, he couldn't decide. Which did he want more? Lillian or his dreams of a large and loving family?

Chapter Eighteen

On Sunday, the bishop and minister preached about Moses and the troubles he and his people endured before they reached the Promised Land. Some lost their faith, others faltered and recovered, but God was with them all along. Lillian knew it was an attempt to raise the spirits of the community, but it did nothing to raise hers.

A collection was taken for the victims of the fires, but the amount raised didn't come close to covering the losses. The bishop assured people he would make appeals to other churches and they had to be content with that. The community had been pushed into poverty in a matter of days. It would take them years to recover.

Lillian avoided seeing Timothy after the service by leaving early. Amanda was upset that she couldn't stay and play with her friends, but Lillian promised she could have a friend come for a sleepover later in the week and that mollified her.

Lillian spent the day writing a long letter to her parents explaining about the fires and the law's inability to find those responsible. She thought of the box in her desk and wondered what she should say to Jeremiah. He hadn't mentioned missing the canisters, and there had been fires set without them. He had to be innocent. She believed that in her soul.

As much as she dreaded facing Timothy on Monday, she was still happy to see his dear face when he walked into the schoolhouse before classes. He didn't mention their last meeting and neither did she. They were polite and kind to each other. It was as if a large and invisible glass wall had been erected between them. She had no idea how to break through without cutting her heart to shreds.

How long could they go on this way?

The children were all quiet and studious. Everyone had been affected by the senseless violence against them. Lillian realized that the joy she felt when she was teaching had vanished, but she owed it to the children to give her best.

On Wednesday night, she was surprised to see Silas Mast at her door. She bade him come in. He stood in her kitchen with his hat in his hands, turning it round and round as he stared at the floor. Unease crept up her spine. "What's wrong, Silas?"

He looked at her then. "You know that our community has been hard hit by these fires. Everyone has emptied their pockets to help one other, and still there are those who will bear a hard financial burden from these events."

"I know that you more than anyone have suffered a great loss," she said kindly.

"The Lord does not give us more than we can bear. However, I must think about the needs of others as well as my own needs. I have met with the school board earlier tonight. We have decided that this district can no longer afford to pay two teachers."

"I see. Have you told Timothy?"

"I came to speak with you first and offer you the job, but I know your family is moving back to Wisconsin and you may wish to go with them."

She had prayed for a sign, and the Lord was showing her a clear path, although not one she expected. But this way she wouldn't have to face Timothy every day and endure the pain of knowing he loved her and she loved him in vain.

"Timothy has proven his worth," she said. "The children adore him. Let him keep the job. You are right. I would like to return to Wisconsin with my family."

He looked relieved at her quick decision. "Will you stay out the month?"

Two more weeks of seeing Timothy every day? Could she do it?

She didn't want to give up one more minute with him, but a clean break would be easier for both of them. "My parents will he home this weekend and we'll be leaving again as soon as possible. Friday must be my last day."

"As you wish. Shall I tell Timothy?"

"I will see him tomorrow. I can do it." She pasted a smile on her face in spite of the pain in her heart.

After the end of school the following day, she shared the news with Timothy. Drawing a deep breath, she kept her gazed pinned to the floor. "I have decided to move with my family." She looked up to see his reaction.

He was clearly taken aback. "You're leaving?"

Lillian hadn't felt so miserable in ages. The bewildered look in Timothy's eyes made her long to cup her hands on either side of his face and tell him none of it was his fault. The fault lay with her alone.

She thought she had accepted God's plan for her life.

To be a teacher, not a wife and mother. To that end, she had hardened her heart against loving any man, but love had crept in unnoticed in the guise of friendship. The friendship of a wonderful, kind and generous man.

"When?" His voice broke on the word.

"This is my last week."

"I see." The resignation in his tone told her more than his words that he wasn't ready to let her go.

"It's for the best. This is too hard."

"I don't know what to say." His eyes bored into hers.

"Wish me well." *Tell me you love me. Ask me not to go.*

"I wish you every good thing, Lillian, you know that. I'll miss you."

"I'll miss you, too."

She saw the glint of tears in his eyes as he left.

Standing in her empty classroom, she raised her eyes to heaven, praying for strength. Someday Timothy would fall in love, marry and, God willing, have children. If she stayed, she would one day teach them in this school. How could she bear it? Why was she being tested this way?

"Lillian, are you all right?" Debra asked softly from the doorway.

"*Nee*, I'm not."

"Can I do something to help?"

"Show me how to fall out of love. Do you have a pill for that?"

"Oh, my poor dear." Debra came and put her arms around Lillian.

Her kindness was the final straw. A raw sob broke from Lillian's throat. It opened a floodgate of tears. Pouring her sorrow out on Debra's shoulder, Lillian was only vaguely aware that Debra led her to a chair and sat down beside her.

When Lillian was done crying, she pulled away from Debra. "I'm sorry."

"Don't be. Tears are good for us."

"I know. We all need puffy eyes and red noses." She sniffed once. "What are you doing here?"

"I came bearing gifts."

"For who?"

"You because I don't know anyone else well enough to give them this." Debra took her bag off her shoulder and pulled out a slip of paper. It was a check for a huge sum of money.

Lillian looked at her in shock. "I can't take this."

"You can and you will. Give it to your bishop to divide it among the people who have lost so much."

"How can you possibly afford to give so large a sum?"

Debra laughed. "You're right. It would take a few years to earn this at my salary. Have you heard of crowd funding?"

Lillian shook her head.

"I shouldn't be surprised, since you don't use a computer. There are internet sites where you post a plea for money and people can donate to your cause if they believe in it."

"People gave this amount? Strangers?"

"Many people gave a little. A few gave a lot. One person gave a whole lot. I'm sure there will be more money coming in as word spreads about this violence against innocent and humble people."

"I don't know what to say."

"I think the word is *danki*," Debra said with a cheesy grin.

"That is the word." Lillian threw her arms around

Debra and hugged her with gratitude overflowing from her heart.

"Now would you like to tell me why I found you in tears? I take it you are in love with someone who doesn't love you back?"

"He does love me, and that is the problem."

"Girl, you are going to have to explain this from the top."

Lillian was sitting at her desk when Timothy came in the next morning. He spoke quickly. "Our chief just told us they know who's been starting these fires."

She quelled the sudden panic in her gut. "Have they said who it is?"

"He wouldn't give a name until an arrest has been made, but it is a local man."

Where was Jeremiah? He hadn't come home last night. How could she help him?

Timothy sat down on the chair beside her. "People will find it hard to accept that it was one of us. You don't look surprised, Lillian."

It was no use pretending anymore. "I have suspected for some time that Jeremiah might be involved."

"What? I can't believe that. Your brother is an honest fellow. What makes you suspect him?"

Lillian unlocked the large bottom drawer of the filing cabinet and pulled out the cardboard box. She took off the lid and set the box on the top of her desk. In it were the three propane canisters she had discovered under her brother's buggy seat. "I don't know what reason Jeremiah has been keeping these. I discovered them by accident under the seat of his buggy. These are the same kind that were used to start the fire at the Hanson Farm and in Bishop Beachy's hayfield, aren't they?"

"I think so."

"What should I do, Timothy? He's my brother and I love him. Your brother made mistakes and he repented. I know Jeremiah is a good man. I don't understand why he would do such a thing. In my heart I don't believe he would, but then I see this evidence."

"You don't have to do anything, sister."

She looked up to see her brother walking toward her. "Jeremiah, what are you doing here?"

"I came to tell you that Davey Mast has been arrested."

The relief that surged to her was short-lived. "What about these?" She gestured toward the propane canisters.

"I took them out of his car. I thought I could prevent him from starting another fire, but that failed. I have tried to convince him to stop, but he wouldn't listen to reason."

She rose and ran to her brother, throwing her arms around his neck. "I never wanted to believe it was you, but you have been acting so strangely."

He returned her embrace. "I'm sorry that I frightened you. I knew what Davey had done, and I have been trying to talk him into giving himself up."

She drew back. "Poor Silas. This will be a terrible blow."

Jeremiah nodded. "Davey was the one who told me that Hanson had fired his boss's crew for stealing tools. He said he could hire an Amish crew to harvest the field for half the price. I thought it was odd, knowing Hanson never cared for us, but I wanted to make some extra money. Davey offered to drive me to the Hanson place before anyone else found out he was looking to hire a new crew. I know I shouldn't have accepted a ride from him, but Davey and I have been friends for years. If Hanson hired us, Davey would work for me and not lose any pay."

"But Mr. Hanson wasn't looking for an Amish crew," Timothy said.

"He started yelling and ordering us off the place. He called Davey a liar and a thief and said the only thing worse than an Amish was an ex-Amish thief. Davey was furious."

Lillian cupped her brother's sad face. "I know his shunning was hard on you."

"I knew there was good in him. I thought I could get him to come back to us. He never meant to put the school and all the children in danger. He said that fire just got out of hand."

"So why did he start the fires at Bishop Beachy's hay-field and why would he burn down his father's barn?" Lillian asked, still trying to wrap her mind around the fact that someone she had known for years could do such things.

Jeremiah shook his head. "I don't know what happened to him. Maybe getting away with the Hanson Farm fire made him think he could do it again. He once told me the bishop should be punished for shunning him. I know his father's refusal to even speak to him hurt him deeply. He honestly did try to keep the fire from spreading by stopping it that day."

"We all thought he was a hero," Timothy said, shaking his head.

"All men are made up of good and evil," Lillian said.

Jeremiah stepped back and held Lillian at arm's

length. "I also came here to tell you that I will be moving to Wisconsin with *Mamm* and *Daed*. There is more work for me there and fewer bad memories."

"I'm coming, too."

He looked from her to Timothy. "Are you sure you want to do that?"

Lillian raised her chin. "It's what I need to do. I have news of my own. Debra and her brother have been fundraising for us. I have a check to deliver to the bishop for many thousands of dollars. Everyone who lost things in the fire will get enough money to help them recover."

Jeremiah tipped his head to the side. "The *Englisch* are sending money to us? *Daed* will never believe it."

"It looks like God has smiled on us after we endured our trials," Timothy said.

She handed the check to her brother. "Will you deliver this to the bishop for me?"

"Gladly. This is wonderful news. All our problems are solved," Jeremiah said as he headed out the door.

Lillian felt the awkwardness return now that she and Timothy were alone. Jeremiah was wrong. Not all their problems had been solved. Could she really leave Timothy?

Chapter Nineteen

Somehow Timothy made it through the weekend, but the pain in his heart never let up. How long would it take him to get over Lillian? A year? A lifetime?

His family was busy with plans to rebuild the gift shop and help with numerous barn raisings. Like most of the community, they were saddened to know the arsonist had once been a member of their faith.

Newspaper reporters and a few television crews came to Bowmans Crossing looking for a story angle. They went away frustrated when the Amish they tried to interview avoided their questions and their cameras.

Monday morning finally arrived. For the first time in his short career, he approached the school with dragging steps. She wouldn't be there today or ever again.

He opened the door. The schoolroom was as empty as his heart without her. He walked across the plank floors, his footsteps echoing softly in the stillness. He stopped in front of her desk. She wasn't coming back. She wouldn't be here to help him learn to be a good teacher. She wouldn't be here to make him smile at her teasing or to share some wonderful new story with. How was he going to go on without her?

He stepped behind the desk and looked out over the empty rows of student desks waiting patiently for the children to arrive. He was their teacher now, and he wouldn't let them down. For such a small woman, Lillian had left him big shoes to fill. The children would miss her, too. He couldn't allow a broken heart to interfere with his most important task.

He pulled out the chair and sat down at her desk. One by one, he opened the drawers searching for some trace of her. He found it in the bottom right drawer. A blue sweater, folded and forgotten.

He pulled it out and pressed the soft wool to his face as he inhaled her fragrance. Tears stung his eyes. He couldn't let her go. He had to find a way to convince her to return.

It didn't matter that they wouldn't have children together. If that was God's plan for them, he would face it with a glad heart if only she would be his wife. How could he make her believe that?

"Timothy?"

He looked up and saw her standing in the doorway with the morning light streaming in around her. He wasn't sure he could trust his eyes. "Lillian? I prayed you would come back."

"I left my sweater here. I came to collect it before I left." She held out her hand.

"You can't have it. I love you, Lillian. Please don't go away. I can't breathe when you aren't near me."

Tears filled her eyes. "Nothing has changed."

"Yes, it has. I've changed. I'm a teacher who needs help. I wanted children, and now I have forty-two of them looking to me for guidance. How can I be all I need to be without you by my side?"

"They won't be your children. Your flesh and blood."

"They will demand blood, sweat and tears from me. From both of us. It's enough for me. Isn't it enough for you? Now that the community has been blessed with such generous donations, I'm sure the school board will hire you back. If they don't, they will have to find another teacher, for I won't stay without you."

She took a step toward him. "I don't want you to settle for something you will regret later."

He walked toward her and took her in his arms. Slowly, she wrapped her arms around his waist. He sighed and laid his cheek on the top of her *kapp*. "I will never regret loving you. How could I? You are the soul mate our Lord God fashioned for me before the earth was made. You complete me."

Her lips trembled. "I'm afraid."

He drew back to look at her face. "Afraid of what?"

"I'm afraid to be this happy."

"Ah, my sweet." He pulled her close again. "I will spend my life making you happy for every year that God gives us. Will you stay?"

Lillian couldn't believe how close she had come to giving up and leaving. One favorite sweater was all that had stood between this happiness and a lifetime of regret. If it hadn't been a misplaced sweater, she would have found another reason to see Timothy for one last time. She thanked God for giving her this wonderful accepting man.

"Okay." She managed a breathless whisper.

"Okay you'll stay?"

She nodded.

"Okay, you love me?"

She nodded again.

"Okay you will marry me?"

"Yes." It was a tiny squeak of a reply, but he heard it and pulled her close.

"Thank you, my sweet, sweet Lillian. You have just made me the happiest man on earth."

She raised her face to his and kissed him with all the passion she'd held inside for so long.

The final day of Silas's barn raising, a semitrailer turned off the highway and came slowly up Silas's lane. It was a cattle hauler. The truck stopped near the newly completed barn where Timothy and his brothers were laying down the shingles. The truck door opened. A small, wry man with a thick gray mustache and a beat-up cowboy hat got out. Lillian was amazed to see he was a little person. She and the Bowman women were setting out the food for the men working, as it was almost noon.

"Howdy, folks. Is this the farm of Silas Mast?" the cowboy asked.

Silas stepped forward and nodded. "It is."

"Would you be Silas?"

"I am."

The cowboy held out his hand and Silas shook it. "Nice to meet you. My name is Barney Mast. I don't reckon we're any kind of kin, as I'm from Oklahoma, but when I saw what you folks had gone through, I was moved to help. You may not know it, but you're the answer to an old man's prayers."

"In what way?"

"I'm a dairyman myself. Been one all my life just like my daddy and granddaddy. My wife has been harping at me to retire for the last five years. We never had any kids, so I didn't have anyone to take over my spread. Know what I mean? Dairy cows are a 24/7 operation. I raised every one of my cows and their mothers and their mother's mothers. I know them like I know the back of my hand. I can sell my land, but I couldn't sell my gals to just anyone, so I brought them here."

Timothy and his brothers had come down and now stood beside Lillian. Silas shook his head sadly. "I'm afraid you have traveled a long way for nothing. I can't afford to buy your herd."

"Oh, I don't want to sell them, but I can sure give them to a man who'll appreciate every last one of them. That you and me share the same last name is just icing on the cake for me. I'd like to get them unloaded. They're gonna need to be milked soon. We've been on the road for near eighteen hours."

"You are giving your dairy herd to me?"

"Yup. I read about the fires and your loss and how you Amish folks take care of one another and I thought that's the kind of people I want looking after my gals."

Silas pulled off his hat and ran his hand through his hair. "I don't know what to say."

"Say thanks and we're even. My wife is tickled pink that I'm finally gonna retire and do some traveling with her. She's been waiting fifty years to see the ocean. I don't understand what's so special about a lot of water, but I'm taking her to Hawaii as soon as I get back."

Lillian leaned against Timothy as tears pricked at the back of her eyes. The Lord did indeed move in strange and wonderful ways.

* * *

Lillian and Timothy's intention to marry was announced to the congregation three weeks after he proposed. The wedding would take place the first Tuesday in November. Lillian expected her friends to be surprised by her engagement, but most of them weren't. Emma said, "We all knew that you two were made for each other. Friends don't look at friends the way you and Timothy look at each other."

A whirlwind of activity began for Lillian the day after the banns were published. Invitations had to be sent as soon as possible so that far-flung relatives and friends could make travel arrangements. She sat with her mother at the kitchen and looked at the stack of envelopes waiting to be addressed.

"I'm glad we don't have a huge family," Lillian said, picking up the first envelope. There were only a few cousins and her great-uncle in Wisconsin. She didn't expect many of them to come, but she hoped they would.

Lillian tucked an invitation inside the envelope and licked it. "Do you think Uncle Arthur will come?"

"If he is well, I'm sure of it," her mother said. "He was always fond of you and I think he wants to make up for the time he lost with us. God was good to give him this second chance."

Lillian smiled. God was indeed good. He'd given her this chance at a lifetime of love with a man who was her best friend. To think she had almost thrown it all away out of pride!

After filling out the first set of invitations, her mother pointed to a group of envelopes already bundled together. "Who are those invitations for?"

"I am sending one to each of the children at school.

Timothy and I want to make sure all of them were included."

"Has Timothy given you his list?"

"He brought it over last night." Lillian concentrated on the card in her hand, hoping her mother wouldn't notice the blush heating her cheeks. She and Timothy had spent a long, happy evening exchanging kisses and talking about their plans for the future.

"Are you inviting the *Englisch* nurse and her brother?"

"Of course. Their intervention and charity made a huge difference to this community."

The pile of invitations was just the start of Lillian's duties. Her days were soon filled with sewing her wedding dress, cleaning, cooking and preparations for the big day. She was thankful she didn't have the added burden of teaching on top of it all. She chose a deep blue material for her wedding gown. She would be married in it and buried in it, as was the custom of her people.

The one thing she didn't like about all the activity was that she saw little of Timothy except at school. The board had happily given her back her job, but she and Timothy rarely found time to be alone for more than a few stolen moments.

The day before the wedding, her married friends and members of the church arrived to prepare the wedding feast and the house for the bridal party. A generous meal would be served following the wedding, but the celebration would continue until evening, when a second meal would be needed for all the guests who remained.

When the day finally arrived, Lillian was up at four thirty in the morning. Anticipation filled her stomach with butterflies. By noon, she would be Timothy's wife.

Closing her eyes, she whispered a grateful prayer thanking God for this wondrous gift.

She went to the window to see the stars shining over a winter wonderland scene. Fresh snow coated everything. Timothy would be up by now. What was he feeling? If she married Timothy, he would never have sons and daughters of his own. What if he came to regret this decision?

Timothy stood at the window of his room gazing out at the bare winter trees silhouetted against the new-fallen snow. Was Lillian up? Was she experiencing the same kind of jitters? Was he doing the right thing? Marriage was forever.

She would be his forever.

He drew a deep cleansing breath. Forever with Lillian wouldn't be enough time to show her how much he loved her.

A tap on the door made Timothy glance that way. It was Luke. "It's time. Noah has the buggy here for you, and the others are ready."

Timothy and Lillian had asked Rebecca and Samuel along with Emma and Luke to be members of the bridal party. Noah was acting as hostler, the driver for the group who would all be traveling to Lillian's house together.

Timothy took another deep breath, and his nervousness vanished. With God's help, he would be a good husband. He would provide for her and cherish her all the days of his life. What had he done to deserve such happiness?

He walked downstairs to see his brothers and his father waiting for him. Samuel gave him a lopsided grin. "Noah wanted me to give you a message."

"What is it?"

"He said he picked the fastest horse in case you change your mind and want to head in another direction."

Their mother bustled into the room. "Nonsense. Timothy is too smart to leave a woman like Lillian waiting at the altar."

"He takes after his mother," Isaac said, patting his wife's plump cheek. She batted his hand away and blushed.

Timothy turned to his oldest brother. "What do you think, Samuel?"

"My advice is to go through with it. When you have found the right woman, being married is *wunderbar*."

"Good answer," Rebecca said, coming into the room from the kitchen with their infant son in her arms. She rose on tiptoe and kissed Samuel. The light in their eyes told Timothy they were still crazy about each other after almost two years. He wanted Lillian to smile at him the way Rebecca and Samuel were smiling at each other, as if they shared some profound understanding.

"I don't know why we are all standing around. I want to get hitched." Timothy opened the door and went out into the clear, cold morning air.

Chapter Twenty

Timothy was waiting for Lillian at the foot of the stairs when she came down. He looked incredibly handsome in his new black suit and bow tie. Her husband-to-be smiled and held out his hand. "Are you ready?"

She grasped his fingers tightly. "I am. Are you? Now is the time to change your mind."

"*Nee*, you are stuck with me, woman."

Her heart turned over with joy. "*Goot*, for I am so happy I'm surprised I'm not floating on air."

He squeezed her fingers. "I will keep you grounded. I will be your anchor."

She gazed into his eyes. "We're going to be all right, aren't we?"

"*Ja*, we are going to be fine."

"We will never have children. I know having sons was important to you."

He smiled at her tenderly. "We will have thirty or forty children for nine months out of the year. That's enough. And if it isn't, we will adopt ten or twelve. There are children who need parents everywhere. God will show us our path. Whatever life brings, we can face it together."

"You are wonderful and wise." She laid a hand on his cheek.

"I don't know about the wise part, but I am wonderful."

"*Demut*, Timothy. Try to be humble for a change."

"Okay. I am a simple man grateful for God's gifts and you are wonderful."

She grinned. "Much better."

They weren't alone for long. A few minutes after seven o'clock, the guests began to arrive. The pocket doors between the rooms had been pushed open, and the benches were being set up by her brother and her father.

Together, Lillian and Timothy greeted the early guests as they came in. The ceremony wouldn't take place until nine. Timothy was happy to see Brandon, his wife and children and Debra walk through the door. These outsiders had been instrumental in getting the families of Bowmans Crossing back on their feet. The two people he hadn't expected were Mr. and Mrs. Hanson.

He shook Mr. Hanson's hand. "It's good to see you looking well."

"My wife tells me I need to be more neighborly. Reckon this is as good a place to start as any."

"We are delighted you could come," Lillian said, giving them a beaming smile.

She motioned to Susan Yoder. "Would you sit by these people and translate for them?"

"Sure. Come this way. I'll seat you in the back where we have some soft chairs."

At a quarter till, the wedding party took their places

on the benches at the front of the room where the ceremony would be held. Lillian, Rebecca and Emma sat on one side of the room, Timothy with Samuel and Luke sat on the other.

Their *forgeher*, four married couples from their church group, escorted the guests to places on one of the long wooden benches. When the bishop entered the room, he motioned for Lillian and Timothy to come with him as the congregation began singing.

It was customary for the bishop to counsel the couple before the ceremony. Lillian and Timothy listened intently to his instructions, but Lillian was too excited to take in much.

When the bishop was finished, she and Timothy returned to where the guests were seated and took their places on the front benches. The singing continued, punctuated by sermons from the ministers, including her father, for almost three hours. Lillian tried to keep her mind on what was being said, but mostly she thought about the coming days and nights when she would become a true wife to Timothy.

Standing in front of Timothy, the bishop asked, "Do you believe, brother, that God has provided this woman as a marriage partner for you?"

"I do believe it." Timothy smiled at her, and her heart beat faster.

The bishop then turned to her. "Do you believe, sister, that God has provided this man as a marriage partner for you?"

"I do."

"Timothy, do you also promise Lillian that you will care for her in sickness or bodily weakness as befits a

Christian husband? Do you promise you will love, forgive and be patient with her until God separates you by death?"

"I do so promise," Timothy answered solemnly.

The bishop asked Lillian the same questions. She focused on Timothy. He was waiting for her answer, too. Taking a deep breath, she nodded. "I promise."

The bishop took her hand, placed it in Timothy's hand and covered their fingers with his own. "The God of Abraham, of Isaac and of Jacob be with you. May He bestow His blessings richly upon you through Jesus Christ, amen."

And with that prayer, they were made husband and wife. Love and happiness spilled out of her heart and flooded her body as she gazed at Timothy. Her overwhelming love was reflected in his eyes and the wonderful smile on his face.

A final prayer ended the ceremony, and the festivities began. The women of the congregation began preparing the wedding meal in the kitchen as the men arranged the tables in a U shape around the walls of the living room. Lillian went upstairs to change out of her wedding dress.

The *eck*, the honored corner table, was quickly set up for the wedding party in the corner of the room facing the front door. When everything was ready, she and Timothy took their places.

He was married. Timothy found it hard to wrap his mind around the fact. He took his place with his groomsmen seated to his right. Lillian was ushered in and took her seat at his left-hand side. It symbolized the place she would occupy in his buggy and in his life. Her cheeks were flushed a rosy red and her eyes sparkled with happiness. There would be a long day of celebration and feasting, but tonight would come, and she would be his alone. Could he make her happy? He would try his best. He reached over and squeezed her hand. She gave him a shy smile in return.

After a very long day, the wedding guests had all gone home at last. Lillian sat at the kitchen table and waited for Timothy to join her. He had gone out to say goodbye to his brothers and see them on their way. The outside door opened and he walked in. Joy rushed through her at the sight of his handsome face.

"Wife, would you care to join me for a short walk this evening? It's a nice night out."

"A walk sounds lovely, my husband."

"Have I told you today how much I love you?" He crossed the room and took her hand, pulling her to her feet and into his arms.

She melted against him, loving the way he made her feel. "You may have mentioned it. I'm not sure."

"Lillian Bowman, I love you. Today, tomorrow, for the rest of eternity. I love you."

Would she ever tire of those words? Never. "I love you, too. What did I do to deserve such happiness?"

"I ask myself the same question. I reckon only God knows the answer."

"He has truly blessed us." She rose on her tiptoes to press a kiss to his lips.

Wrapping his arms around her, he pulled her closer and kissed her until her head was spinning and she was breathless. Pulling away, he took a deep breath. "Maybe that walk can wait."

Sliding her arms around his neck, she snuggled against him. "Yes, my husband. I've waited to be in your arms for long enough. Kiss me again."

He smiled and gave her a quick peck on the lips. "I will always do what the teacher tells me."

* * * * *

If you enjoyed HIS AMISH TEACHER, look for
the other books in the AMISH BACHELORS series:
AN AMISH HARVEST
and
AN AMISH NOEL.

Dear Reader,

I hope you have enjoyed this new story in the Amish Bachelors series. The Bowman brothers have all been fun to write about. I have used my four brothers as inspiration for many of their quirks and conversations.

The story of the arsonist in this book was inspired by true events. In 1993 the grandson of an Amish bishop was arrested and charged with setting fires to multiple Amish farms in one night. As with my story, the damage was too costly for the Amish community to absorb. After a newspaper article detailed their struggles, donations poured in for them to the point that they had to return some money.

People are basically good, be they Amish or English. As Lillian said, every man has good and bad within him.

Blessing to all,

Patricia Davids

COMING NEXT MONTH FROM
Love Inspired®

Available March 21, 2017

HER SECRET AMISH CHILD
Pinecraft Homecomings • by Cheryl Williford

Returning to her Amish community, Lizbeth Mullet comes face-to-face with her teenage crush, Fredrik Lapp. As he builds a bond with her son and she falls for him all over again, will revealing the secret she holds turn out to be their undoing—or the key to their happily-ever-after?

THE COWBOY'S EASTER FAMILY WISH
Wranglers Ranch • by Lois Richer

Widowed single mom Maddie McGregor moved to Tucson, Arizona, for a fresh start with her son. She never expected Noah's healing would be helped along by the former youth minister working at Wranglers Ranch—or that Jesse Parker could also be her hope for a second chance at forever.

EASTER IN DRY CREEK
Dry Creek • by Janet Tronstad

Clay West is back in Dry Creek, Montana, to prove he's innocent of the crime he was convicted for. But when he reconnects with old friend Allie Nelson, his biggest challenge will be showing her not only that he's a good man—but that he's the perfect man for *her*.

WINNING OVER THE COWBOY
Texas Cowboys • by Shannon Taylor Vannatter

When Landry Malone arrives in Bandera, Texas, to claim her inheritance of half a dude ranch, co-owner Chase Donovan plans to run her out and keep his family legacy. Landry is just as determined to show the cowboy she's up for the challenge of running the place—and winning his heart.

WILDFIRE SWEETHEARTS
Men of Wildfire • by Leigh Bale

As a hotshot crew member, Tessa Carpenter is always ready to fight wildfire. Yet nothing could've prepared her for having her ex-fiancé as her boss. Sean Nash's guilt over Tessa's brother's death caused him to end their engagement. Now he's bent on getting back the love of his life.

THEIR SECOND CHANCE LOVE
Texas Sweethearts • by Kat Brookes

Hope Dillan is back in Texas to help her ailing father recover. Making sure his nursery business stays afloat will mean working with Logan Cooper—the sweetheart she's never forgotten. To embrace a future together, can she finally reveal the secret that tore them apart?

LOOK FOR THESE AND OTHER LOVE INSPIRED BOOKS WHEREVER BOOKS ARE SOLD, INCLUDING MOST BOOKSTORES, SUPERMARKETS, DISCOUNT STORES AND DRUGSTORES.

LICNM0317

Get 2 Free Books,
Plus 2 Free Gifts—
just for trying the Reader Service!

Love Inspired.

"Lie still. You may have broken something," Lizbeth instructed.

His hand moved and then his arm. Blue eyes—so like her son's—opened to slits. He blinked at her. A shaggy brow arched in question. Full, well-shaped lips moved, but no words came out.

She leaned back in surprise. The man on the ground was Fredrik Lapp, her brother's childhood friend. The last man in Pinecraft she wanted to see. "Are you all right?" she asked, bending close.

His coloring looked normal enough, but she knew nothing about broken bones or head trauma. She looked down the length of his body. His clothes were dirty but seemed intact.

The last time she'd seen him, she'd been a skinny girl of nineteen, and he'd been a wiry young man of twenty-three. Now he was a fully matured man. One who could rip her life apart if he learned about the secret she'd kept all these years.

He coughed several times and scowled as he drew in a

deep breath.

"Is the *kinner* all right?" Fredrik's voice sounded deeper and raspier than it had years ago. With a grunt, he braced himself with his arms and struggled into a sitting position.

Lizbeth glanced Benuel's way. He was looking at them, his young face pinched with concern. Her heart ached for the intense, worried child.

"*Ya*, he's fine," she assured Fredrik and tried to hold him down as he started to move about. "Please don't get up. Let me get some help first. You might have really hurt yourself."

He ignored her direction and rose to his feet, dusting off the long legs of his dark trousers. "I got the wind knocked out of me, that's all."

He peered at his bleeding arm, shrugged his broad shoulders and rotated his neck as she'd seen him do a hundred times as a boy.

"That was a foolish thing you did," he muttered, his brow arched.

"What was?" she asked, mesmerized by the way his muscles bulged along his freckled arm. It had to be wonderful to be strong and afraid of nothing.

He gestured toward the boy. "Letting your *soh* run wild like that? He could have been killed. Why didn't you hold his hand while you crossed the road?"

Don't miss
HER SECRET AMISH CHILD by Cheryl Williford,
available April 2017 wherever
Love Inspired® books and ebooks are sold.

www.LoveInspired.com